I0609149

Joseph Ashby-Sterry

Boudoir Ballads

Second Edition

Joseph Ashby-Sterry

Boudoir Ballads
Second Edition

ISBN/EAN: 9783744787949

Printed in Europe, USA, Canada, Australia, Japan

Cover: Foto ©Andreas Hilbeck / pixelio.de

More available books at **www.hansebooks.com**

BOUDOIR BALLADS.

BY

J. ASHBY-STERRY,

AUTHOR OF " TINY TRAVELS," "SHUTTLECOCK PAPERS," ETC.

SECOND EDITION.

London

CHATTO AND WINDUS, PICCADILLY.

1877.

[*The Author reserves all rights of Translation and Reproduction.*]

CONTENTS.

THE KEY-NOTE.

I take the dainty quill of dove,
  A baby harp of joy:
I pen the lightest phase of love,
  I sing the fragile toy.

I rave about a damsel's dress
  And versify on lace;
I burnish gold on tiny tress,
  And praise a pretty face.

I'd pen a fancy for a flirt,
  And rhyme on Beauty's bills;
Or write a sonnet on her skirt,
  A Laureate of Frills!

A

MY LADY'S BOUDOIR.

I.

HER Boudoir is a charming oasis,

'Mid dull arid deserts of life ;

'Tis the elegant haunt of the Graces

Set free from society's strife ;

'Tis a haven of rest amid trouble—

When the prism of fashion has flown—

O'er the wreck of the froth of the bubble

My Lady can ponder alone

II.

She can tell to her love-birds her sorrow,

    When no interloper is nigh ;

She may hope for the joy of to-morrow,

    Or hopelessly have 'a good cry !'

Ah, what dreams she can dream in the twilight!—

    When no longer acting a part—

In that exquisite mystical shy light,

    What truth she may tell to her heart !

III.

Far away from all prying beholders,

    Their praise or their blame she may flout ;

She may shake her bewitching white shoulders,

    Or sulkily grumble and pout !

She may take crumpled notes from her pocket,

    And study them oft by the hour ;

She may muse o'er a face in her locket—

    Sigh over a poor faded flow'r.

IV.

In her moments of grief or dejection,
  (Her life without these may not pass),
She'll reflect on the tearful reflection—
  A pretty sad face in the glass !
Or when dimpled bright Joy may have kist her
  As Love comes his darling to claim—
She will smile on her pretty twin sister,
  Who smiles upon her from the frame !

V.

'Tis an elegant chamber and cosy,
  In taste it is simple and true,
And its rich window-curtains are rosy,
  Its walls are of *céladon* hue :
They are hung with Du Maurier's sketchings
  Of satire of *salon* or street,
And with Rajon and Whistler's etchings
  And favourite *cartes de visite.*

VI.

Just a touch of the craze chinacratic
   Is shown in those Staffordshire mugs ;
In the plates, with their dragons erratic,
   And curious Japanese jugs.
In the quaint old Majolica fishes,
   The hideous Indian elves,
And the rare Dresden figures and dishes,
   That stand on the Chippendale shelves.

VII.

See the chairs, like to couches of heather ;
   The carpet, like moss to the tread ;
And the screen of choice Cordovan leather,
   The sofa as soft as a bed ;
The quaint mirrors that came from Murano,
   The skins of the chamois and sheep,
With the daintiest little piano,
   And lounges that lull you to sleep.

VIII.

There's a clock with bright blossoms for numbers,
　　And minutes enamelled in blue,
With old Time, scarce awake from his slumbers,
　　Reposing on rich *ormolu ;*
Golden pointers are silently chasing—
　　Quite deaf to the argentine ring—
They loiter not once in their racing,
　　Tho' Beauty may sorrow or sing !

IX.

Can she stay that old scythe with her treasure ?
　　Can flowers hide fugitive Time ?
Is the knell of each fast-fading pleasure
　　Tolled sweeter by silvery chime ?
She may cheat herself, if she is able,
　　And play with the enemy tricks—
' Rose past lily ' is only a fable,
　　It means but a quarter past six !

X.

Would you look at the varied selection
　　Of books, in this snug little spot?
See the authors who gain her affection,
　　With Thackeray, Dickens, and Scott?
Tho' Minerva she fancies a bore is,
　　She loves those who laugh when they teach—
See the volumes of verses and stories,
　　The scrap-book of sketches by Leech.

XI.

See her desk with its elegant litter
　　Of letters half penned and half read ;
With the Genoese inkstand a-glitter,
　　Where petals of roses are shed :
See her half-opened purse and her papers,
　　A glove and some charms on a chain,
And the seals and the rose-coloured tapers,
　　Her keys and a steel *châtelaine.*

XII.

See the basket of work half completed,
  The braiding that's hardly begun,
And the pictures so girlfully treated,
  The sketches all brimming with fun :
See the Cupids that clamour for kisses—
  Well drawn by a dear little maid—
And the work of Old Masters, young misses
  Have thrown for a time in the shade !

XIII.

'Tis the pleasantest place in the Spring-time
  To lounge thro' the bright sunny hours,
When we hope longer days may soon bring time
  All gay with new bonnets and flow'rs ;
When the chesnuts at Bushey are snowy,
  And Hope brighter destiny weaves,
When the hyacinth-glasses are showy,
  And Nature turns over new leaves.

XIV.

Ah ! a chat in this chamber so nice is,

　　When girls twine their tresses with blue,

And make bets on the Cam and the Isis,

　　And worship their favourite crew ;

When Spring, with her touch talismanic,

　　Leaves Winter to desolate doom ;

And the tent at the breezy Botanic

　　Is rich in a revel of bloom !

XV.

When sweet May, with a bountiful measure,

　　Rains down her bright blossoms in showers ;

And when duty seems almost a pleasure,

　　And life nought but sunshine and flowers !

When the dawn of the Season's unclouded—

　　As London is once more alive—

With the Opera daintily crowded,

　　And thronged are the Row and the Drive.

XVI.

How they dote on each merry May Meeting—

 I don't mean at Exeter Hall—

But the gossip, the chatter and greeting

 Pervading each concert and ball;

The words that are whispered in waltz-time,

 To butterfly flutter of flirts;

When fairy feet falter in false time,

 To *frou-frou* of feminine skirts!

XVII.

Ah! the days down at Ascot delicious,

 The skies of forget-me-not blue;

And those meetings, of course adventitious,

 On Sunday, so oft, at the Zoo.

O the ceaseless flirtation and chatter!

 What tales one could tell, if he durst,

Of the loves that are lost at the latter,

 The gloves that are won at the first!

XVIII.

Then the mornings of picture reviewing
    Within the Academy walls ;
And the terrible headaches ensuing,
    The worry of callers and calls !
Ah ! the scent of the violet blending,
    With ballad some beauty may sing—
Chords of sound and of perfume transcending,
    The magical music of Spring !

XIX.

'Tis a bower of bliss in the Summer,
    When swallows sing low in the eaves,
And the advent of any fresh comer
    Is hymned by the music of leaves ;
When the air with sweet perfume is laden,
    And quiver the gay stripen blinds ;
When the bright blushing cheek of each maiden
    Is kissed by the soft summer winds !

XX.

How they reckon each joyous occasion,

  Where bright sunny hours shall be spent,

And make plans for a girlish invasion

  To lunch in some Wimbledon tent ;

If their frills should be wide worn or narrow,

  If skirts should be lengthy or short ;

Of the chances of Eton and Harrow,

  Or being presented at Court.

XXI.

Then their partners they praise and disparage,

  Or fling back their soft scented hair,

And talk over the latest good marriage

  And dresses at Hanover Square.

How they prattle without rhyme or reason !

  Or, hushed in some dainty day-dream,

They will hum the last waltz of the season,

  Or banquet off strawberry-cream !

XXII.

Then how gladly each overdanced martyr

 Will give up her ' afternoon Park,'

Just to dine at the dear ' Star and Garter,'

 And snugly drive home in the dark !

How the light in bright eyes brighter kindles,

 As darlings will joyfully vote,

To run down to luncheon at Skindle's,

 And moon up to Marlow by boat !

XXIII.

O the boredom at old Lady Quince's !

 Whose dinners are terribly slow,

O the rapture of rinking at Prince's !

 Tho' wheel is a prelude to woe.

O the joy of a crisp early canter !

 The lounge in the Park 'neath the trees :

And the gossip, the scandal, and banter,

 And fun at the Hurlingham teas !

XXIV.

When my Lady is dreamily playing,
    What fancies she'll oft improvise !
As her dimpled white fingers are straying
    In ecstacy over the keys !
And the eyes of your *innamorata*
    Remind you such moments are fleet—
As she plays you the ' Moonlight Sonata,'
    Or sings to you ' Summer is Sweet ! '

XXV.

'Tis a glorious lounge in the Autumn,
    When girls show a longing to roam,
And declare that the swallows have taught 'em
    'Tis time to be flitting from home !
When the pink on the peach almost matches
    The bloom on the cheek of my fair,
And the gleam on the corn nearly catches
    The hue of the gold in her hair !

XXVI.

When the sun of the Season is setting—

 As London her legion disbands—

When each beauty quits ball-room coquetting,

 For flirting on Scarborough sands !

When Terpsichore's own picaninny—

 As Fashion unshackles her slaves—

Leaves the music of Coote and of Tinney,

 For singing of surf· sighing waves !

XXVII.

They are full then of bustle and hurry,

 And long to be off on their flight ;

For they read nought but *Bradshaw* and *Murray*

 And guide-books from morning till night.

They pant for the worry and clatter

 Of *diligence*, railway and boat,

And they long for the polyglot chatter

 Endured at each gay *table d'hôte !*

XXVIII.

They are ripe for the roughest exertion,
And talk about doing Mont Blanc,
As they dream of the Alpine excursion,
The mule and the slow *char-à-banc;*
Or of rising, when daylight is dawning,
In Italy's climate divine;
And of dinner on deck, 'neath the awning,
By vine-clustered hills of the Rhine!

XXIX.

O the vision of girlish distresses,
The pitiful pouting of pets!
As they chat over ' knock-about' dresses,
And talk over thick ulsterettes!
Ah! the chorus of maidens ecstatic,
Who long for the Chamouni pines;
For a glimpse of the blue Adriatic,
Or sight of the rich Apennines!

XXX.

O the picture of packing and pleasure,
  The flutter that reigns in the nest!
And the mixture of labour and leisure—
  The days full of bustle and rest.
As the Queen of the flitting unravels
  New plans for the pluming of wings;
Or perchance slumbers o'er 'Tiny Travels,'
  Or sweetly 'The Vagabond' sings.

XXXI.

'Tis the snuggest retreat in the Winter,
  When dreary and short are the days;
When the beech-billets crackle and splinter,
  When ruddy and bright is the blaze;
When the room is deliciously mellow—
  Weird shadows come fast as they go—
And the ceiling is chequered and yellow,
  And gloom gives a glory to glow.

B

XXXII.

When the lamp, with its shade opalescent,

　To chestnut turns bonny brown curls,

And the laughter of maids effervescent

　Wells up from the prattle of girls !

Then their wisdom seems nothing but folly,

　But folly seems almost divine,

When lips laugh at the red of the holly,

　And mistletoe hangs as a sign !

XXXIII.

In the midst of this weather hibernal

　Will beauty indulge in a pique?

Will she find an enjoyment supernal,

　In patience, in chess, or *bézique ?*

Or perchance with sheer laziness smitten

　She has nothing then left to desire—

If she curls like her own Persian kitten,

　And basks in her fur by the fire !

XXXIV.

She may sit with her feet on the fender,
  And gaze upon dainty kid shoes ;
She may grow sentimental and tender,
  Or sing off a fit of the ' blues.'
She may muse there in dreamy quiescence—
  A Gheber you see at a glance—
And read in the logs' incandescence,
  A world of the wildest romance.

XXXV.

Ah ! what plans for the passing of slow time
  Some fur-coated beauty imparts,
As she sighs for the sleighing in snow-time,
  And laughs at the slaying of hearts !
For this sweet little siren in sable—
  Who looks so bewitchingly nice—
Is as willing, as ready and able,
  To tempt us on dangerous ice !

XXXVI.

How she longs for the hyaline ice-time
  And musical ring of the skate !
As she plays with sweet feeling and nice time
  ' Les Patineurs,' from *Le Prophète.*
Or with Dickens's grand Christmas stories
  She dreams in the close-curtained bay,
And forgets in their magical glories
  The dull Christmas-tide of to-day.

XXXVII.

You may listen to plots histrionic
  For whiling long evenings away,
With charades or a *proverbe* laconic,
  Some *tableaux*, a concert or play :
And you'll hear how mere novices hanker—
  With faith in their untested pow'rs—
To attempt to play Lady Gay Spanker,
  Or e'en Mary Netley in *Ours !*

XXXVIII.

There's something omitted. I know it,

  And own it at once when I say,

If I had but the pen of a poet,

  And magical brush of Millais,

I should feel I'd neglected no duty—

  As sadly I say *Au revoir*—

Forced to leave undescribed the chief beauty

  That reigns in My Lady's Boudoir.

PET'S PUNISHMENT.

I.

IF my love offended me,
   And we had words together,
   To show her I would master be,
I'd whip her with a feather !

II.

If then she, like a naughty girl,
   Would tyranny declare it,
I'd give my pet a cross of pearl,
   And make her always bear it.

III.

If still she tried to sulk and sigh,

And threw away my posies,

I'd catch my darling on the sly,

And smother her with roses !

IV.

But should she clench her dimpled fists,

Or contradict her betters,

I'd manacle her tiny wrists

With dainty golden fetters.

V.

And if she dared her lips to pout—

Like many pert young misses—

I'd wind my arm her waist about,

And punish her—with kisses !

IN A BALCONY AT BARNES.

8th April 1876.

I.

NO prudish professors from Girton,
  Altho' they're a couple of 'blues,'
Who know more of rowing 'tis certain
Than strong-minded Beckerite 'views.'
Such beauties seem made to be petted—
  So smiling, bewitching, and bright,
So daintily gloved and rosetted,
  Such Queens of the Dark and the Light!

II.

They prattle of 'smartness of feather,'
    And talk about 'winning the toss ;'
They chatter of 'keeping together,'
    Of errors in 'steering across.'
Each feels that her own crew is winning,
    And speaks of a 'glorious spurt ;'
They know that to 'catch the beginning,'
    Is good for a rower—or flirt !

III.

When blue blades flash past on the river,
    Then anxious are blue-bedight girls :
In bosoms forget-me-nots shiver,
    And violets nestle in curls !
They breathlessly wait for the crisis—
    As boats hurry fast to the mark—
Will Cam throw a pallor on Isis ?
    Or tears turn light ribbons to dark ?

IV.

Then pull for the pride of the river—

For tiny cerulean glove,

For droplets of turquoise that quiver

In ears of the girl whom you love ;

For the *lazuli* bracelet that presses

The wrist of your own little pet,

For glory of azure-twined tresses—

Pull hard for the blonde and brunette !

V.

When oarsmen have ceased their appliance,

When finished the muscular fight,

Will pluck and Oxonian science

Be conquered by 'sweetness and light?'

Though Fortune you fancy capricious,

'Twill scarcely be cause for surprise,

If violet's perfume delicious

Be vanquished by bright watchet eyes

REGRETS.

I.

FOR the look of those pure grey eyes—
  Seeming to plead and speak—
The parted lips and the deep-drawn sighs,
  The blush on the kissen cheek!

II.

·O for the tangle of soft brown hair,
  Lazily blown by the breeze;
The fleeting hours unshadowed by care,
  Shaded by tremulous trees!

III.

O for the dream of those sunny days,
   With their bright unbroken spell,
And the thrilling sweet untutored praise—
   From the lips once loved too well!

IV.

O for the feeling of days agone,
   The simple faith and the truth,
The spring of time and life's rosy dawn—
   O for the love and the youth!

TWO AND TWO:

A Song of School Girls.

I.

COME the little ones in frocks,
　With their broidered knickerbocks,
　And their tangled sunny locks—
　　　Laughing crew !
Come the dimpled darling pets,
With their tresses all in nets,
And their snow-white pantalettes
　　　Just in view :

Come the gay and graceful girls,

With their chignons and their curls—

Sweetest string of Beauty's pearls,

>   Two and two !

II.

What delicious laughter trills,

When rude Boreas half wills,

Just to flutter fairy frills

>   All askew !

And as petticoats are short,

Frequent glimpses may be caught—

Though p'r'aps this may be naught

>   Unto you—

Of small, deftly booted feet,

Of slim legs and ankles neat,

Passing by you much too fleet

>   Two and two !

III.

On the Book of Beauty's page

Fairer girls of ev'ry age,

Skilful artist, I'll engage,

      Never drew.

Tender Ten may dote on toys,

While for Twelve jam tarts have joys,

Feat Fourteen's in love with boys—

      Not a few ;

And sweet, bonny, bright Sixteen

Wears an arch coquettish mien,

As they walk upon the Green

      Two and two !

IV.

Here the coming flirt appears,

With the belle of after-years,

And the beauty even peers

      May pursue :

Each Lilliputian fair

Gallant Guardsmen may ensnare,

Or enthral a millionaire,

             And subdue !

Who would think such mischief lies

In the future of their sighs,

Or such pretty childlike eyes—

                Two and two ?

v.

There are eyes of peerless brown,

That in time may take the town ;

There are others drooping down—

             Black or blue—

Whose bright flashes you may find

Will be-dazzle—nay, may blind—

E'en the wisest of mankind,

                False and true.

Pouting lips we cannot miss,

Sweet foreshadowings of bliss—

Which, in truth, seem made to kiss

        Two and two !

VI.

When school studies are all done,

And life's lessons have begun,

And rich lovers, one by one,

        Gladly sue :

When each bright-eyed little pet,

Leaves De Porquet for Debrett ;

Or perchance a coronet

        Comes to woo—

They have learnt, for after-life,

That the husband and the wife

Should together face its strife

        Two and two!

WEARY.

I.

'M sick of the world and its trouble,
   I'm weary of pleasures that cloy,
   I see through the bright-coloured bubble,
   And find no enjoyment in joy.

II.

Is all that we earn worth the earning?
   Is all that we gain worth the prize?
   Is all that we learn worth the learning?
   Is pleasure but pain in disguise?

III.

Is sorrow e'er worth our dejection?

Is fame but a flatterer's spell?

Is love ever worth our affection?

Le jeu vaut-il, donc, la chandelle ?

IV.

O where are the eyes that enthralled us,

And where are the lips that we kissed?

Where the siren-like voices that called us,

And where all the chances we missed?

V.

We know not what mortals call pleasure—

For clouded are skies that were blue;

To dross now has melted our treasure,

And false are the hearts that were true.

VI.

The flowers we gathered are faded,
  The leaves of our laurels are shed ;
Our spirit is broken and jaded,
  The hopes of our youth are all dead.

VII.

We feel life is hopeless and dreary,
  Now night has o'ershadowed our day ;
Bright fruits of this earth only weary,
  They ripen—to fall and decay !

VIII.

I'm sick of the world and its trouble,
  For rest and seclusion I thirst ;
I'm tired of the gay tinted bubble,
  That brighteneth only to burst !

NUMBER ONE.

PORTRAIT OF A YOUNG LADY,

'No. 1,' in a collection of one thousand five hundred and eighty-three works of art, at the Exhibition of the Royal Academy.

1.

MY favourite, you must know,

In the Piccadilly Show,

Is the portrait of a lass

Bravely done.

'Mid the fifteen eighty-three

Works of art that you may see,

There is nothing can surpass—

'Number One!'

II.

Very far above the line
Is this favourite of mine ;
　　You may see her smiling there
　　　　O'er the crowds.
If you bring a good *lorgnette,*
You may see my dainty pet ;
　　Like the Jungfrau, pink and fair,
　　　　'Mid the clouds.

III.

My enchanting little star,
How I wonder what you are,
　　With your rosy laughing lips
　　　　Full of fun.
Have you many satellites,
Do you shine so bright o' nights,
　　That there's nothing can eclipse
　　　　' Number One ? '

IV.

Are you constant in your loves?

Do you change them with your gloves?

    Pray does Worth pervade your train—

        Or your heart?

Are you fickle, are you leal,

Are your sunny tresses real,

    Or your roses only vain

        Works of art?

V.

I sincerely envy him

Who the fortune had to limn

    Your bewitching hazel eyes

        With his brush:

Who could study ev'ry grace

In your winsome little face,

    And the subtle charm that lies

        In your blush.

VI.

I am sure it is a shame

That your pretty face and frame,

    Ruthless hangers out of view

        Seek to hide :

But no doubt Sir Francis G—

And his myrmidons agree,

    Peerless angels such as you—

        Should be ' skyed ! '

VII.

Ah ! were I but twenty-two,

I would hinge the knee to you,

    And most humbly kiss your glove

        At your throne :

Thrice happy he whose sighs

Draw this sweet Heart Union prize

    In the lottery of Love

        For his own !

VIII.

If I knew but your papa,

Could I only ' ask mama,'

It is clear enough to me

As the sun,

That all through this weary life,

'Mid its pleasure, pain, and strife,

All my care and love should be

' Number One.'

FALSE OR TRUE?

TRUTH frequently lies, I've oft heard tell,
  In deepest depths of a deep, deep well:
  Can you imagine it always lies
In fathomless depths of sweet brown eyes?

THE TWO MOTHERS.

First Picture.

I.

SHE loves the *gandin's* vapid stare,

And praise from all beholders—

Adopts the latest tint in hair,

And whitens thick her shoulders !

Her smiles are perfect works of art,

And Worth makes all her dresses ;

Her love comes from a hollow heart—

From Brittany her tresses.

II.

Her sallies and her *jeux d'esprit*
  Throughout the town are quoted,
For trenchant speech and repartee,
  Madame is vastly noted.
She cares not for the love of girls—
  Nor minds if they deride her—
Her ponies equal Cora Pearl's,
  Her pearls out-Schneider Schneider !

III.

She sees her children now and then
  With tolerant compassion ;
Perchance she'll learn to love them when
  Maternity's the fashion.
A childlike kiss her bloom might spoil,
  The dimpled hand of Mignon
In baby-play might chance uncoil
  The fabric of her chignon.

By the Seine, 1868.

Second Picture.

I.

In sunny girlhood's vernal life
  She caused no small sensation ;
But now the modest English wife
  To others leaves flirtation.
She's young still, lovely, debonair,
  Although sometimes her features
Are clouded by a thought of care
  For those two tiny creatures.

II.

Each tiny, toddling, mottled mite
  Asserts with voice emphatic,
In lisping accents, ' Mite is right.'
  Their rule is autocratic :

The song becomes, that charmed mankind,

   Their musical narcotic,

And baby lips, than Love, she'll find,

   Are even more despotic !

III.

Soft lullaby, when singing there,

   And castles ever building—

Their destiny she'll carve in air,

   Bright with maternal gilding :

Young Guy's a clever advocate—

   So eloquent and able—

A powdered wig upon his pate,

   A coronet for Mabel !

By the Thames, 1874.

DAISY'S DIMPLES.

I.

LITTLE dimples so sweet and soft,
　　Love the cheek of my love :
The mark of Cupid's dainty hand,
　　Before he wore a glove.

II.

Laughing dimples of tender love
　　Smile on my darling's cheek ;
Sweet hallowed spots where kisses lurk,
　　And play at hide and seek.

III.

Fain would I hide my kisses there

At morning's rosy light,

To come and seek them back again

In silver hush of night.

IN STRAWBERRY TIME.

I.

NOT, hot glows the sunshine in laughing July,

    Scarce flutter the leaves in the soft summer

        sigh :

The rooks scarcely swing on the tops of the trees,

While river-reeds nod to the odorous breeze :

A rose-leaf, a-bask in the sunshiny gleam,

Half sleeps in the dimples that chequer the stream ;

The dragon-fly hushes his day-dreamy lay,

The silver trout sulks in his sedge-shaded bay—

While our thoughts sweetly run in a soft singing rhyme,

As we lazily loiter in strawberry time !

D

II.

Sweet, sweet is the scent of the newly-mown
    hay,

Light borne by the breeze on a bright summer's
    day ;

And cool is the sound of the musical plash,

As bright bubbles fall in the fountain and
    flash.

'Tis joy then to wander in gay golden hours,

And dream 'mid the hues of the bright-tinted
    flow'rs ;

When the velvety lawn is most soft to the tread,

And ruddy fruit hangs in the leaf-covered
    bed—

Then the roundest, the sweetest, the best of the
    prime,

Will we gather together in strawberry time !

III.

Joy, joy 'tis to whisper and laugh in the
    shade,

And pluck the ripe fruit for my hazel-eyed
    maid;

To watch her delight as she eagerly clips

A pink British Queen with her soft pouting
    lips!

While lovingly gazing I'm apt to compare

The warm blushing berries with lips of my
    fair;

I'm doubtful, indeed, if the fruit of the South

Could equal the charm of her ripe little
    mouth—

'Tis so round and so soft, 'twould be scarcely a
    crime

All my doubts to dispel in sweet strawberry time!

IV.

Light, light is the laughter that carelessly
rings,

And sweet is the carol she tenderly sings !

I murmur a story we all of us know—

Her soft dainty dimples, they come and they
go ;

Her eyelids droop down o'er those sweet
little eyes,

Her laughter is hushed in a tumult of sighs :

Those pretty, plump fingers, red-stained to the
tips,

All tremble, while pouting are rosy-red
lips.

Then the bard whispers low, 'neath the tremulous
lime,

" Lips sweeter than fruit are in strawberry time ! "

A LOVER'S LULLABY.

I.

MIRROR your sweet eyes in mine, love,
　　See how they glitter and shine !
　　Quick fly such moments divine, love,
　　　Link your lithe fingers in mine !

II.

Lay your soft cheek against mine, love,
　　Pillow your head on my breast ;
While your brown locks I entwine, love,
　　Pout your red lips when they're prest !

III.

Mirror your fate, then, in mine, love ;

Sorrow and sighing resign :

Life is too short to repine, love,

Link your fair future in mine !

TOO TRUE.

I.

'TIS over! It is done at last!
   The fetters Cupid forges
     Were riveted quite hard and fast,
       Last Monday, at St. George's.
A shoddycrat with ample means,
   A priest intoning neatly,
A bishop and two rural deans,
   Have tied the knot completely.

II.

And so you're on your honeymoon,
  And wear a golden fetter;
You speculate—'tis rather soon—
  "Is it for worse or better?"
You're thinking of a year ago—
  'Twas just such sunny weather—
But somehow time went not so slow
  When we two were together.

III.

A year ago, those pretty eyes
  A world of truth reflected;
A year ago, your deepest sighs
  I never half suspected:
A year ago, my tale I told,
  And you were glad to listen;
You were as pure, as good as gold,
  Or any maid fresh kissen.

IV.

In life's brief play you chose your part,

    Poor little foolish vendor!

You sold your trustful loving heart

    For shoddy and for splendour.

The sky so blue, the sea so glad,

    Brings joyous recollections;

And yet you seem a world too sad

    For honeymoon reflections!

LITTLE CHINCHILLA.

𝔄 Symphony in Fur.

I.

SHE wears the shortest skirts,
 And shows the whitest frilling;
She looks—as Queen of Flirts—
 Miraculously killing!
She'll skim the thinnest ice,
 As light as Queen Camilla,
She looks supremely nice—
 My little pet Chinchilla!

II.

The sleekest otter cuffs—

   The rosiest of real skin—

The sable-est of muffs—

   The softest gloves of sealskin.

The quaintest hose with clocks,

   A cloud like a mantilla,

The velvetest of frocks—

   Wears little sweet Chinchilla !

III.

O should the gracious fates

   But deign to be propitious ;

I strap her fairy skates,

   On furry boots delicious.

Her willing hand I take—

   In spite of Aunt Priscilla—

Then speed I o'er the lake,

   With little love Chinchilla !

IV.

The warmth of her regard
    I take as sort of token—
Although it's freezing hard—
    Our social ice is broken !
Coquettish in her furs—
    She minds not my Manila—
Ah ! what a glance is hers,
    My little dear Chinchilla !

V.

She'll figure, glide and twirl,
    And worry the officials ;
She'll cut out ev'ry girl,
    As easy as initials !
O I could skate for miles—
    Or dance a seguidilla—
Cheered by the sunny smiles
    Of little smart Chinchilla !

IV.

Had I enough a year,
  To find my sweet in sable,—
To wrap my dainty dear
  In ermine were I able,—
Had I a longer purse,
  A neat suburban villa,—
For better or for worse
  I'd take my pet Chinchilla.

BLANKTON WEIR.

A Water-side Lyric.

I.

'TIS a queer old pile of timbers, all gnarled and
rough and green,

Both moss-o'ergrown and weed-covered, and jaggëd
too, I ween!

'Tis battered and 'tis spattered, all worn and knocked
about,

Beclamped with rusty rivets, and bepatched with
timbers stout;

A tottering, trembling structure, enshrining memories
dear,

This weather-beaten barrier, this quaint old Blankton
Weir.

II.

While leaning on those withered rails, what feelings

oft come back,

As I watch the white foam sparkling and note the

current's track;

What crowds of fleeting fancies come dancing through

my brain !

And the good old days of Blankton, I live them o'er

again;

What hopes and fears, gay smiles, sad tears, seem

mirrored in the mere,

While looking on its glassy face by tell-tale Blankton

Weir !

III.

I've seen it basking 'neath the rays of summer's golden

    glow,

And when sweetly by the moonlight, silver ripples

    ebb and flow;

When Nature starts in spring-time, awakening into

    life;

When autumn leaves are falling, and the yellow corn

    is rife;

'Mid the rime and sleet of winter, all through the

    live-long year,

I've watched the water rushing through this tide-worn

    Blankton Weir.

IV.

And I mind me of one even, so calm and clear and

bright,

What songs we sang—whose voices rang—that lovely

summer night.

Where are the hearty voices now who trolled those

good old lays?

And where the silvery laughter that rang in bygone

days?

Come back, that night of long ago ! Come back, the

moonlight clear !

When hearts beat light, and eyes were bright, about

old Blankton Weir.

E

v.

Was ever indolence so sweet, were ever days so
  fine,

As when we lounged in that old punt and played
  with rod and line?

'Tis true few fish we caught there, but the good
  old ale we quaffed,

As we chatted, too, and smoked there, and idled,
  dreamed, and laughed:

Then thought we only of to-day, of morrow had no
  fear,

For sorrow scarce had tinged the stream that flowed
  through Blankton Weir.

VI.

Those dreamy August afternoons, when in our skiff

    we lay,

To hear the current murmuring as slow it swirled

    away;

The plaintive hum of dragon-fly, the old weir's plash

    and roar,

While *Some-one's* gentle voice, too, seems whispering

    there once more;

Come back, those days of love and trust, those times

    of hope and fear,

When girls were girls, and hearts were hearts, about

    old Blankton Weir!

VII.

Those brilliant sunny mornings when we tumbled
out of bed,

And hurried on a few rough clothes, and to the river
sped !

What laughing joyaunce hung about those merry days
agone,

We clove the rushing current at the early flush of
dawn !

'Tremendous headers' took we in the waters bright
and clear,

And splashed and dashed, and dived and swam, just
off old Blankton Weir.

VIII.

Then that pleasant picnic-party, when all the girls
were there,

In pretty morning dresses and with freshly-braided
hair ;

Fair Annie, with the deep-blue eyes, and rosy, laughing Nell,

Dark Helen, sunny Amy, and the Howard girls as
well ;

Ah ! Lizzie, 'twas but yesterday—at least 'twould so
appear—

We plighted vows of constancy, not far from Blankton
Weir.

IX.

Those flashing eyes, those brave true hearts, are gone,
and few remain

To mourn the loss of sunny hours that ne'er come
back again :

Some married are—ah ! me, how changed—for they
will think no more

Of how they joined our chorus there, or helped to
pull the oar :

One gentle voice is hushed for aye—we miss a voice
so dear—

Who cheered along with evensong our path by
Blankton Weir.

X.

Amid the whirl of weary life, its worry and its

bore,

Comes back that well-loved lullaby—the old weir's

distant roar:

It gilds the cloud of daily toil with sunshine's fitful

gleams,

It breaks upon my slumber, and I hear it in my

dreams:

Like music of the good old times, it strikes upon

mine ear—

If there's an air can banish care, 'tis that of Blankton

Weir!

XI.

I know the river's rushing, but it rushes not for

   me,

I feel the morning blushing, though I am not

   there to see ;

For younger hearts now live and love where once we

   used to dwell,

And others laugh, and dream, and sing, in spots we

   loved so well ;

Their motto ' *Carpe diem* '—'twas ours for many a

   year—

As show these rhymes of sunny times about old

   Blankton Weir.

THE SEVEN AGES OF GIRLHOOD.

I.

AT Two, she is a tiny lass,
  And joy she scarcely knows from sorrow;
She scarce consults her looking-glass;
  She has no thought of sad to-morrow!

II.

At Four she is a merry maid,
  And looks on aught but play as folly;
She can't believe bright flowers fade—
  That only sawdust is her dolly.

III.

At Eight, her troubles come in scores,

    For oft she is perverse and haughty;

A pouting puss in pinafores—

    Who's sometimes whipped when she is naughty!

IV.

At Twelve, she is a saucy teaze,

    Who knows full well her glances rankle;

Her petticoats scarce veil her knees,

    And fairy frills scarce kiss her ankle.

V.

At Fifteen, she's the pearl of.pets,

    And feels assured her pow'r is strengthened;

Her snowy school-girl trouserettes

    Are hidden when her skirt is lengthened.

VI.

At Sixteen, she's the sweetest sweet,

    And dresses in the height of fashion ;

She feels her heart 'neath bodice beat,

    In earnest for the tender passion.

VII.

At Eighteen, p'r'aps she may be sold

    Her lot to share, for worse or better ;

She'll either sell her heart for gold—

    Or give it for a golden fetter !

ZOOLOGICAL MEMORIES.

I.

AH, Dora, my darling, can your recollection
　　Revert to a Sunday once early in June?
When leaving your Aunt's ever-watchful protection,
　　You saucily said you'd 'come back again soon,
But must see the seal and the spotted hyena,
　　And doted on zoöphytes scarlet and blue,'—
Poor Aunt left at three, and at six we'd not seen her—
　　That bright summer Sunday we met at the Zoo.

II.

You wore, I remember, the nicest of dresses,
　　So simple and fresh, though it would not compare

With Miss Buhl's splendid train, while your sunny
>   bright tresses
>   Could never out-rival her ' Brittany' hair :
Her parasol shaded the costliest bonnet—
>   'Twas gorgeous and showy, 'twas heavy and new ;
While yours was of lace, with blush roses upon it,
>   That gay summer Sunday we lounged in the Zoo.

III.

You recollect loitering down by the water—
>   I mean by the pond where the pelicans dwell—
A small glove was pressed, it was six and a quarter,
>   A hand rather smaller was p'raps pressed as well ;
You said it was nonsense, and would not believe me—
>   I vowed, on my honour, 'twas perfectly true—
Those lashes down-drooping could never deceive me,
>   That sweet summer Sunday we passed at the Zoo.

IV.

While strolling around that green pond edged with
  rushes—
  I wished we could wander for miles and for miles—
Your eyes brightly shone, whilst the loveliest blushes
  Flushed cheeks dimpled o'er by the sweetest of
  smiles.
Then archly you said, with the sweetest of glances,
  ' Who flirted at Prince's with Lily and Loo?
What makes you so churlish at dinners and dances,
  When you can be so nice when we meet at the
  Zoo?'

V.

How swift flew the hours as we wandered together,
  Forgetful of Aunt as she sat in the shade !
'Twas really too bad in that broiling hot weather ;
  And when we returned what excuses you made !

'Past six, Aunt? It can't be! You surely are
    joking—

We've not seen the zebra nor red kangaroo!'

Then prettily pouting, you looked so provoking,

    That fine summer Sunday we roamed at the Zoo.

VI.

While bright autumn leaves in the country are falling,

    And London is empty, the butterflies flown ;

That sunshiny Sunday I can't help recalling,

    As I sit in dull chambers and ponder alone.

And now you are down at 'The Larches,' my treasure,

    To find short days long, for there's nothing to do,

Does ever come o'er you with exquisite pleasure

    The thought of that Sunday we loved at the Zoo?

A TRAVELLER'S TARANTELLA.

Written in 'Murray's Handbook,' while the band in the Piazza San Marco was playing the Tarantella from Masaniello.

I.

ALL that the tourist can dream of or hear about,

Crowds on your sight as you carelessly peer about,

Quaint water streets you so carefully steer about,

    See the Rialto, and Square of St. Mark !

Floating in gondolas, laughing and jollity,

Cyprian wine of the very best quality,

At Florian's *caffè*—mid fun and frivolity—

    Venice delightful from daylight to dark !

      Musicians in plenty,

      Play '*Ecco ridente,*'

Or ' *Com'e gentil,*' in the still summer night ;

If you're in a hurry,

Pray look in your *Murray*—

You'll find his description is perfectly right !

II.

Albergo Reale and English society,

Bric-à-brac shops in their endless variety,

Plenty of pigeons not fearful of pie-ety,

Flutter and peck 'neath the bluest of skies.

Dreaming in Venice ?   Ah, wildest of fallacies—

Bronzes and sculpture, mosaics and chalices,

Convents and churches and prisons and palaces,

See as you stand on the grim Bridge of Sighs !

The ballads of Byron,

You'll find will environ

The Doges and dodges and Brides of the Sea.

Don't get in a flurry,

But read it in *Murray*—

If you don't care about it, then listen to me !

F

III.

Thousands of thirsty mosquitoes are biting one,

Silvery moonlight is ever delighting one,

Music and mirth every moment inviting one—

    Dreary old London we quickly forget !

Shylock and Portia—in short, the whole kit of 'em,

Readers of Shakespeare recall ev'ry bit of 'em ;

Troublesome guides, you can never get quit of 'em—

    Pictures by Titian and old Tintoret !

       The sock and the buskin,

       With Rogers and Ruskin,

Are mixed in a muddle with palace and sight !

       It may be a worry,

       But don't forget *Murray,*

He'll throw on your darkness some excellent

    light !

CAFFÉ FLORIAN, VENEZIA.

MAIDS OF THE MALLET.

I.

IF courtly old Watteau now wielded the palette,
>How dainty the pictures his brush would have
>>drawn !
>Could he but have seen the sweet Maids of the
>>Mallet
>Who flutter and flirt on our velvety lawn !

II.

'Tis down by the Thames where the summer wind
>bloweth,
>Just serving to shiver the tremulous trees,
Where sleepy reeds bend to the ripple that floweth, ·
>Scarce deigning to nod to the somnolent breeze.

III.

For *croquet*, the game, I have no admiration,

But who, in his senses, could ever refuse

To hammer his toes in a quiet flirtation

With one of these daintily-booted *croqueuses?*

IV.

The bright eye of Beatie send shafts that will rankle,

The smile of sweet Camille it comforts and kills;

You never, I'm sure, saw a neater-turned ankle

Than peeps from 'neath Jennie's white fanciful

frills.

V.

A part of our game I will give you a hint on—

If you're thirsty, and hanker for something and

ice—

A bountiful beaker of boraged Badminton

You will find, in the shade, is uncommonly nice!

VI.

Deep draughts from the two-handed, dew-clouded
    chalice,
  While musing alone, is most sweet, 'tis confessed ;
But sweeter than all to drink after sweet Alice,
  And kiss the same silver her pouting lips pressed !

VII.

'Tis rapture to lounge in such exquisite clover,
  To bask in the sunshine of Gwendolen's eyes !
With light-hearted Milly to be a gay 'rover,'
  Or 'spoon' to the music of Rosalie's sighs !

VIII.

These Maids of the Mallet, they shake out their
    tresses—
  While men gather round at their siren-like call—
And artfully loop-up diaphanous dresses,
  To break stalwart hearts as they'd *croquet* a ball !

NINA'S NECKLACE.

I.

I HAVE brought the string of pearls
　For my prettiest of girls:
　Let your merry laughter ring !
　　Do not reck
The wild ripple of your hair,
On your dimpled shoulders bare—
　As I clasp the sheeny string
　　Round your neck !

II.

Here are sixteen snowy pearls,

Glad to nestle in your curls,

   Round your neck they closely cling

      With delight—

Fitting emblem of your years,

Free from sorrow, care and tears :

   Sixteen summers softly sing,

      Pure and bright !

III.

Though your sweetest sunny smiles,

And your winsome girlish wiles,

   Right and left you gaily fling—

      Merry miss !

From your lips I claim reward—

If you'll graciously accord ?—

   I will clasp the snowy string

      With a kiss !

SAINT MAY:

A City Lyric.

I.

S T. ALOYS the Great is both mouldy and grim,

The Decalogue's dusty, the windows are dim;

Not knowing the road there, you'll long have

to search

Before you discover this old City church;

Yet often on fine Sunday mornings I stray,

To see a new saint, whom I've christened St. May.

II.

The one bell is cracked in its crazy old tower,

The sermon oft lasts rather more than an hour ;

The parson is prosy, the clerk eighty-three,

The organ drones out in a sad minor key ;

Yet quickly the moments I find fly away,

I pass every week at the shrine of St. May.

III.

Of saints I've seen plenty in churches before—

In Florence or Venice they're there by the score ;

Agnese, Maria—the rest I forget—

By Titian, Bassano, and brave Tintoret :

They none can compare, though they're well in their
  way,

In maidenly grace with my dainty St. May.

IV.

She sits in a high, ancient, black oaken pew,

Which almost conceals her fair face from my view;

The sweetest of pictures it can't be denied,

With two tiny sisters who sit by her side,

Who lisp the responses, or kneel down to pray,

With little hands locked in the palm of St. May.

V.

She's young for a saint, for she's scarcely eighteen,

And ne'er could wear peas in those dainty *bottines;*

Her locks are not shaven, and 'twould be a sin

To wear a hair-shirt next that delicate skin;

Save diagonal stripes on a dress of light gray,

Stripes ne'er have been borne by bewitching St.

    May.

VI.

She's almost too plump and too round for a saint,

With sweet little dimples that Millais might paint ;

Without mediæval nor mortified mien,

Or wimple of yellow, or background of green—

A nimbus of hair throws its sunshiny ray

Of glory around the fair face of St. May.

VII.

What surquayne or partlet could look better than

My saint's curly jacket of black Astracan ?

What coif than her bonnet—a triumph of skill—

Or alb than her petticoat edged with a frill ?

So sober, yet smiling—so grave, yet so gay,

O where is a saint like my charming St. May?

VIII.

The sermon is finished, the blessing is o'er,

The sparse congregation drift out at the door;

I pause, as I stroll down the gloomy old aisle,

To see my saint pass, and perchance get a smile:

I'd almost change faith, like the Vicar of Bray,

To pass all my life in adoring St. May.

IX.

I wend my way home to my chambers alone,

And sunshine is gone and the summer seems flown;

But then does a vision of brightness arise,

Of pureness and truth in those eloquent eyes;

For not a mere picture nor image of clay,

To worship by rubric, is gentle St. May.

X.

Through the weary, dull week, as it rolls on apace,

I'm haunted by thoughts of that tender young face ;

I dream of her spirit, so yielding and kind,

Her goodness of heart, and her pureness of mind ;

And I long for the hour, and count on the day,

To sit at a distance and gaze on St. May.

XI.

No doubt you'll be vastly surprised when you're told

Her name in the Calendar is not enrolled—

They prattled of ' May,' the sweet sisterly pair,

I added the ' Saint,'—she was canonized there.

If saints might wed sinners, I'd yield to her sway,

And straightway would fall on my knees to St. May !

MAIDEN MOUNTAINEERS.

A Sketch at Chamouni.

I.

LOOK at the strong little smart Alpine climbers,
  Sated with scrambles o'er rivers and rocks
(Whose titles would puzzle the craftiest rhymers),
  Proud of their *crampons* and red knickerbocks !
Brown are their hands and right ruddy their faces.
  Hear them discourse on the mountains they've
    'done' !
Watch the delight of their muscular graces,
  Voting the *glissade* most exquisite fun !

II.

Edelweiss laughingly lurks in their tresses—

 Though pretty, they're plucky as Balmat the Bold—

Daintily decked in the darlingest dresses,

 They smile at the danger and laugh at the cold!

Hear them dilate upon *glaciers* and passes,

 Peaks they have scaled, the expert little dears!

Snowstorms are naught to these limber young lasses,

 Chamois are shamed by these fair mountaineers!

PRINCESS POPPY.

A Sleepy Song.

I.

'NEATH the spreading trees in the garden
    glade,
   Where the poppies nod in the chequered
    shade,
In a silken hammock she pouts and lies,
And smiles as she lazily droops her eyes;
As the rook, the brook, and the dragon-fly
Combine in an exquisite lullaby—

        In calm July.

II.

The daintiest dryad who softly sings

To the sweet leaf-music, and slowly swings;

A delicate form and a sweet young face,

Lips parted in exquisite girlish grace.

A more perfect picture you'd ne'er descry,

'Neath the rustling leaves and the summer sky

In fair July!

III.

She smiles as the zephyr her cradle rocks,

With poppies atwine in her golden locks;

She sighs and slumbers to song of the stream,

And slumbers and sighs through a languid dream;

Ah! pray who can tell me the reason why

This beauteous maiden in dreams should sigh,

In sweet July?

G

A COMEDY.

Prologue.

'TWAS all over between us, you thought, when
we parted,
　'Twas good-bye to me and to trouble or care;
A sigh and a tear, a poor boy broken-hearted,
　Was naught, for what feelings had you then to
　　spare?
'Twas nothing to you that my best hopes were
　shattered,
　You knew all the time that you meant we should
　　part;
With fair words did *you* think I e'er could feel flattered,
　From lips feigning truth with such falseness at
　　heart?

ACT I.

Ah, lovely and lost one, I muse in the gloaming,

  And think of one midsummer twilight last year,

But one little year past, when we two were roaming

  With hand locked in hand by the still solemn mere.

Have *you*, love, forgotten that night and those pledges,

  Half-whispered, half-sobbed, 'neath that calm sum-

     mer sky?

In fancy I hear the faint shiver of sedges,

  And still the low plash of the water seems nigh.

ACT II.

You've made, what the world calls, a capital marriage

  Your dinners are perfect, your dances the rage;

They talk, at the clubs, of your new pony-carriage,

  And sneer at your husband, who's double your age:

Ah! fairest of false ones, I'd have you remember,

  Though blooming and bright be the freshness of May,

'Twill tremble before the cool breath of December,

  'Twill silently droop and then wither away

Act III.

They tell me you're happy; and yet, on reflection,

 I find they talk more of your wealth than of you;

And if you have moments of thought and dejection,

 It may be those moments are known but to few,

You've rubies and pearls and a brilliant tiara;

 You breakfast off Sèvres of the real *bleu du Roi;*

'Tis better no doubt than a heart, *mia cara,*

 And a poor posey ring, with its ' *Pensez à moi ?* '

Act IV.

Nay, blame not your husband, nor think you're used

  badly,

 'Twas simply a matter of money and trade;

You named him your ' figure,' he paid it too gladly,

 Your heart was no part of the bargain he made.

He purchased a wife to embellish his table,

 To humour his whims and obey his behests,

One lovely and clever, one willing and able—

 To prove his good taste and to talk to his guests.

Act V.

At times, when 'mid riches and splendour you languish,

　To still your poor conscience you fruitlessly try ;

As tears are fast falling in bitterest anguish,

　You'll own there *is* something that money can't buy.

Yes, love, there are mem'ries e'en gold cannot stifle,

　The ghost of a dead love that will not be laid ;

And while in the bright world of pleasure you trifle,

　Do you never meet the sad eyes of the shade ?

ADIEU TO MABEL.

𝔄 𝔜𝔬𝔲𝔫𝔤 𝔏𝔞𝔡𝔶 𝔄𝔤𝔢𝔡 𝔗𝔢𝔫.

I.

GOOD-BYE, little shock-headed rosy-cheeked
    May,
    Farewell to your tales and your teaching :
Good-bye to your songs and your fairy-like
    play,
    Adieu to your prattle and preaching !

II.

Those eloquent sermons we heard with surprise,
    From lips so enthrallingly simple :
You blinded our reason with light from your eyes,
    And vanquished our hearts with a dimple !

III.

Why can't you remain a sweet ruddy-lipped child,

With bright tangled tresses free-flowing?

To carelessly carol bewitchingly wild,

For pray what's the use, pet, of growing?

IV.

Your laughter has never been saddened by sighs,

You wot not of care or of sorrow,

And tears have ne'er flooded your honest grey eyes

For grief that may come on the morrow.

V.

Good-bye, then, to sweet little sunny-haired pet.

She goes with our best wishes laden:

The light-hearted child we can never forget,

Will live in the lovable maiden!

CLOVER.

I.

DOWN by quiet river-reaches,
　　'Neath the spreading oaks and beeches,
'Mid the stately woods of Clieveden, hard by Maiden-
　　　　head to rest :
　　When sweet summer winds are blowing
　　O'er the grand old Thames swift flowing—
Then a picnic of all parties is undoubtedly the
　　　　best.

II.

You may possibly ride over,

And you'll find yourself in clover,

With the dearest little dryades beneath the shady

trees :

Who can mix a lobster salad

Or troll out the latest ballad,

Who can flirt or pull a pair of sculls, all equally with

ease !

III.

You can stroll down by the river,

Where the nodding sedges shiver,

Or make yourself quite useful carving fowls and

pigeon pies :

You can uncork endless bottles,

Just to moisten parchëd throttles—

Look unutterable language into winsome watchet

eyes !

IV.

When you're weary of the riot,

And may like to have some quiet,

Or to watch the peasants binding up the newly-reapen

sheaves ;

You can hear the oak-trees rustle,

Far away from noise and bustle,

And can whisper silly nothings to the music of the

leaves !

V.

Some-one's glance perhaps grows brighter,

And perchance her heart beats lighter

(I've good reason for supposing that you wander not

alone) —

There's a charm in morning dresses,

And in loosely-braided tresses,

And I hear that magic power lurks in Clicquot and

ozone !

VI.

In a sweet day-dream you wander,

'Neath the chequered shade, and ponder

Beyond the sight and hearing of the old folks and the

rest ;

All your earnest conversation

Is for *Some-one's* delectation—

And I should not be astonished if a little hand were

prest !

VII.

Then, when pales the sunset splendid

As the day is almost ended,

When shadows soft of eventide come stealing up the

glade ;

Her sweet undefined expression

Gives a half-concealed confession,

You've made some small impression on a dainty little

maid !

A BUTTERFLY BALLAD.

I.

SMILE, dainty little beauty,
　　And sing your sweetest song;
　　Think pleasure but a duty,
　　And carol all day long!
The garden's green and shady,
　　And gay are golden hours;
Come then, my gentle lady,
　　To gather fairest flow'rs!

II.

Away fling care and sorrow,
  Be ever bright and gay;
Lose sight of dull to-morrow,
  In sunshine of to-day!
Though brightest blossoms shatter,
  And lovely girls must fade—
To you what does it matter,
  My merry little maid?

PETS OF THE 'PETREL.'

I.

LOUNGING at ease in the laziest attitude,
    Fresh briny breezes are blowing so free;
Never once thinking of longi—or lati—tude,
    Whilst our swift schooner skims over the

    sea.

II.

Smart little sailor-girls, laughing deliciously,
    Soften the skipper with maidenly wiles;
Climb where they oughtn't to, pouting capriciously,
    Vanquish the boatswain with sunniest smiles.

III.

If a squall blows—as it will most unluckily—

 Dear little damsels, the best of A. B.'s,

Face the salt spray, reef their petticoats pluckily,

 Laugh at wet jackets and sing in the breeze!

IV.

Note them, ye maidens so silly and finical,

 See the brown hands of each nautical dear;

Hear them discourse on a bobstay or binnacle,

 Watch their delight when permitted to steer!

V.

E'en at the pumps they would take their turn steadily,

 Though they are maidens be-dimpled and soft;

Sweet little 'salts' do their duty so readily,

 Reef, 'bear a hand,' or would go up aloft.

VI.

Dinners on deck are divinely delectable—

    Under the awning, well screened from the sun—

Some folks would dine *à la Russe* and respectable ;

    Give *us* the laughing, the quaffing, and fun !

VII.

Dreaming when heats of the noontide so hazily

    Shimmer around our becalmed little craft ;

Smoking and mooning, so languidly lazily,

    Whilst some one reads 'neath the awning abaft.

VIII.

Popping at seagulls the girls say is villany,

    ' Cruel and brutal ' they're heard to declare—

Though if by chance you are lucky and kill any,

    Proudly the feathers they'll hasten to wear.

IX.

Dreaming in soft summer night so mysterious,
    Watching the waves as they dash from the bows;
Prattle becoming first sober, then serious,
    Laughter soon softened to tremulous vows.

X.

Drifting from chaff into 'something particular,'
    Though you intended but simply to 'spoon:'
Starlight is good for confession auricular,
    Lunatics thrive in the light of the moon !

XI.

Down in the cabin at night, you most willingly
    Cluster to hear, round the small pianette,
Sweet voices warble low, tender and thrillingly,
    Siren-like songs that you fain would forget.

H

XII.

Far from the boredom of vapid society,

    Leaving all care and all worry at home,

Swift speed the days in an endless variety,

    While the trim 'Petrel' flies over the foam !

LUCY'S LIPS.

 YOUR rosy little mouth—
Red as coral from the South—
Though meant not, Love, for missing
     Quirk or quip:

Was expressly formed, I guess,
For some other lips to press,
What mortals call, Love, kissing
     Lip to lip !

MY VALENTINE.

I.

I LOVE not the sweetest of love protestations
    Emblazoned by artists on paper of snow ;
    The amorous glances and forced suspirations,
      You purchase for money from Cupid & Co.

II.

Those pink chubby boys, with their impudent faces,
    Their hearts and their darts and their old stock-in-
        trade,
Bedizened with tinsel, embowered in laces,
    Shan't bear my love-song to my tender-eyed maid.

III.

Shall hireling muses e'er sing of her splendour,

 Or trumpery poet at twopence a line?

Shall e'er be a bookseller's shopman the vendor

 Of pæan of praise to my sweet Valentine?

IV.

I strike my own harp when I sing to my treasure,

 I'll sing my own song or for ever be still;

And watch her eyes sparkle with exquisite pleasure

 At soft-spoken words which so easily thrill!

V.

I won't bring a harp, and I won't speak in numbers;

 We'll sit as of yore in the snug-curtained room;

When old folks are taking post-prandial slumbers,

 We'll dream by the fire 'twixt the glow and the
  gloom!

VI.

When sunny-brown tresses, in firelight, gleam golden,
    And ripple down soft o'er a bosom of snow;
When a dear, little waist is more closely enfolden—
    There's sweetness in silence we both of us know!

VII.

Carissima mia, I don't mind confessing,
    While soft silken love-locks I fondle and twine,
Though you tremble and blush, I can scarcely help
        pressing,
    That white little hand warmly nestled in mine!

VIII.

There's thrilling expression in tightly-locked fingers,
    And music in whispers half broken by sighs.
In soft dainty dimples a kiss-print still lingers,
    While love gladly lurks in those violet eyes.

IX.

Away with all tears, not a vestige of sorrow
  Shall chequer these moments so sweetly divine !
In sunny to-day I'll not dream of to-morrow,
  But whisper my love to my own Valentine.

X.

Then O for the rapture to whisper through tresses,
  Soft scented, atwine round those shell-tinted ears ;
Away with all doubts and away with distresses,
  And perish the fancy of sorrow and tears.

XI.

Now, darling, pray tell me if this is not better
  Than commonplace verses one can't understand ?
Than parcel, or picture, or overgrown letter,
  Duly stamped and despatched through St. Martin's-
    le-Grand ?

XII.

Then leave such devices to boarding-school misses,

Who love through the post at a distance of miles ;

I like to make love 'midst a shower of kisses,

And press pouting lips till they're softened to smiles !

AN APRIL SERMON.

I.

FAIR Florence is a butterfly
  Who loves the brightest flow'rs,
    But she will pout and fret and sigh
    E'en during passing show'rs;
When sunbeams gild each golden curl,
  She'll carol light and gay,
But O! I fear she's not the girl
  For any rainy day!

II.

There's Isabel, the sweetest pet,
　　And fairest of the fair ;
She'll trifle with a coronet,
　　Or jilt a millionaire :
A brown-eyed, bonny, cool coquette—
　　Brave hearts she will betray—
Their owners she will quite forget
　　On any rainy day !

III.

Sweet Geraldine in summer days,
　　Is just the girl for me ;
Her smiles are then beyond all praise,
　　Her heart is full of glee :
But had she not her Arab steed,
　　Her Lady's Mile in May,
I fear she would look dull indeed
　　On any rainy day !

IV.

I fancy Rene might be true,
    She's such a little dear;
If I had an estate or two,
    And thousands ten a year !
A Dresden china little dear,
    But not the sort of clay
To form the idol I'd revere
    On any rainy day.

V.

Majestic Maud would fix her throne
    In lordly hall or park ;
She could not love for love alone
    A Foreign Office clerk :
A little house in Camden Town,
    Her lover's little pay,
I fear would make my lady frown
    On any rainy day !

VI.

Proud Ethel is the sort of queen
   At Opera to reign;
To show her jewels flashing sheen,
   And rich brocaded train:
She ne'er could wear a muslin dress,
   Nor 'cab it' to the play;
She's not the girl, I must confess,
   For any rainy day!

VII.

I know a pet of eighteen years,
   Who, true in joy and pain,
Will sweetly smile through falling tears,
   Like April sun through rain:
Whose sky-blue eyes most brightly shine
   When clouds are coldest grey—
I'd like to call that beauty mine
   On any rainy day!

VIII.

I would that she were close to me,

    I'd read her eyes, and then,

P'r'aps to this simple homily—

    She'd sigh a sweet ' Amen :'

How sunny life's sad monotone,

    Illumined by this ray !

With such a darling for my own

    On any rainy day !

OFF AND AWAY!

𝔄𝔫 𝔄𝔲𝔤𝔲𝔰𝔱 ℜ𝔢𝔤𝔯𝔢𝔱.

1.

O the gay London season is over!
   I wished it would come o'er again,
   When the night that you started for Dover,
   I bade you good-bye at the train.
I am doomed by the lateness of session
   In London all autumn to stay,
Through its heat, and ennui, and oppression,
   Whilst you, love, are off and away.

II.

How your pretty eyes drooped just at starting !

   You promised to send me your *carte,*

And I gave you 'Two Kisses' at parting—

   I mean the new novel by Smart.

Not a moment for quiet flirtation—

   The guard his white ensign unfurled—

As the train was just leaving the station,

   I gave you my heart and the 'World.'

III.

You are off amid vineyards and mountains,

   Where myrtle is mingled with maize ;

Where the olive o'ershadows bright fountains

   You'll dream through the fine autumn days ;

Where the roseate sunset is flushing

   Its gleam o'er the amethyst lake,

Whilst the blue ripples seem to be hushing

   To slumber the shore where they break.

IV.

You remember the day at Chiavenna
    We mounted the rugged inclines?
And the sail that we took to Varenna?
    The luncheon we had 'neath the vines?
Vino d'Asti spumante, agoni—
    With bright eyes to flash o'er the cheer.
At the inn of Signora Marcionni,
    The sunniest day of last year.

v.

Then that night at Baveno, whilst smoking,
    When *Some-one* lit my cigarette,
To be found by mama 'twas provoking—
    Your eyes flashed a tearful regret:
How she bore you away in a hurry,
    Despite all excuse I could make!
And said, quoting from odious *Murray*,
    'Night air was so bad by the lake.'

VI.

Will you dream 'neath a snowy umbrella,

    With Tauchnitz each hot afternoon ?

Will you go to the Isola Bella,

    Or row by the light of the moon ?

Will you lounge 'neath the pink oleander,

    Comparing this year with the last ?

Will you e'er in the garden meander,

    And think with regret of the past ?

VII.

When the fragrance of flowers is lightly

    Awaft on the soft evening breeze,

Whilst the pale moon is shining so brightly

    And sweet is the music of trees,—

Will you muse, in that clear autumn weather,

    With feelings of pleasure and pain ?

Will you stroll where we wandered together,

    To wish but last year back again ?

I

VIII.

Perhaps memory's clearest reflection
  Will mirror your future ; but yet
You may dwell on with tender affection
  That night I can never forget ;
When I would have said something, but wavered—
  How quickly such chances slip by !—
Ah ! my darling, had I been so favoured,
  Pray what would have been your reply ?

LITTLE UNDINE.

I.

APRIL is sunshine and sadness;

   'Tis like a fair girl when she cries!

A tinge of sweet sorrow in gladness,

   A brightness in tear-bedewed eyes!

The rain, in a pattering cadence,

   Falls fast upon pathway and street;

It fearfully soaks pretty maidens,

   And ruthlessly splashes their feet.

Behold her, my beauty, *la bella*,

   Of aqueous fairies the queen

With smart little silken umbrella,

   My darling, my little Undine!

Just watch her step over a puddle,

   Regardless of milliners' bills,

When all is confusion and muddle

   And spattered are snowiest frills.

When darlings in otter and sable,

   So sopped are their jackets and curls,

To class them you're clearly unable

   As pretty drowned kittens or girls!

Behold her, my darling so dapper,

   A sweetie of supple sixteen,

In neat little waterproof wrapper,

   My darling, my little Undine!

Behold the bright spherules prismatic,

    That saucily spangle her hair!

She scoffs at all terrors rheumatic;

    She's shod with most exquisite care.

She laughs and will carol and chatter—

    Through clouds seeing patches of blue—

Not heeding the soft April patter,

    Not caring for getting wet through!

Behold her, my lady of showers,

    My fay in a splashed crinoline;

My goddess of rainbows and flowers,

    My darling, my little Undine!

LONDON-BY-THE-SEA.

I.

 BRIGHTON in November
   Is what one should remember,
    When from town so dull and foggy we all
     of us would flee ;
   Where air is pure and bracing,
   The breezes we are facing,
   Away the blues there chasing—
At our London-by-the-Sea.

II.

The morning's plunge at Brill's there,

It scares away all ills there,

How dull or sad or sober you may ever chance to be ;

The sunshine bright is flashing,

While in the water splashing,

Away dull care you're dashing—

At bright London-by-the-Sea.

III.

You're sure to find collected

On pier a crowd protected

From weather as they listen to a symphony in B:

'Neath crystal screen's flirtation,

Scarce screened from observation,

You'll find with consternation—

At gay London-by-the-Sea.

IV.

Grave judges there and jokers,

With actors and stock-brokers,

With every sort of person of high and low degree ;

Professor of art fistic,

And preacher ritualistic,.

With poet wild and mystic—

At brave London-by-the-Sea.

V.

O'er downs to madly scamper,

Without a care to hamper—

'Tis just the thing to do you good I think you'll quite

agree :

All worry you are crushing,

Your blood is gaily flushing,

As off you're swiftly rushing—

At light London-by-the-Sea.

VI.

With Amazons fast going,

Such tangled tresses flowing,

Such skirts and dainty ribbons in breezes blowing

free :

What joy to canter faster

With beauties of the castor,

· As humble riding master,

At smart London-by-the-Sea.

VII.

Then frequently there passes

An army of school lasses,

So full of buoyant spirits and of gladsome girlish glee

That when they softly patter

The *pavé* o'er and chatter,

I'm as mad as any hatter—

At fair London-by-the-Sea.

VIII.

Some take a modest tiffin,

On bun or Norfolk biffin,

At Streeter's or at Mainwaring's, but that will not suit

me,

Though folks may call me glutton

I do not care a button,

But love a lunch with Mutton—

At this London-by-the-Sea.

IX.

The flys are slow and mouldy,

As ev'ry one has told ye,

Its shrimps by far the finest you could ever wish for

tea ;

Its shops are rare and splendid,

Where ev'rything is vended

Till money's all expended—

At dear London-by-the-Sea.

X.

If spirits you would lighten

Consult good Doctor Brighton,

And swallow his prescription and abide by his decree :

If nerves be weak or shaken

Just try a month with Bacon,

His physic soon is taken—

At our London-by-the-Sea.

A RIVER RHYME.

I.

FAR, far from the town,
I spied drifting down,
,Cheeks ruddy and brown—
　　　　Eyes so blue—
A sweet sailor-girl,
With hair all a-curl—
　　　　In canoe.

II.

She dreams in her boat,

And sweet is the note

That white little throat

     Carols through :

She languidly glides,

And skilfully guides—

     Her canoe.

III.

'Neath tremulous trees,

She loiters at ease,

And I, if you please

     Wonder who

May be the sweet maid,

Who moons in the shade—

     Inconnue.

IV.

O pray who can tell,

Is she Nina or Nell?

Or Beatie or Bell?

      Is she Loo?

The laziest pet,

You ever saw yet—

      In canoe.

V.

The river's like glass—

As slowly I pass,

This sweet little lass,

      Raises two

Forget-me-not eyes,

In laughing surprise—

      From canoe.

VI.

And as I float by,

Said I 'Miss, O why?

O why may not I

     Drift with you?'

Said she, with a start,

'I've no room in my heart—

     Or canoe!'

SNOWFLAKE.

I.

ONE Christmas down at Beaumont Hall—
  'Twas vastly pleasant, I remember—
The happy moments I recall
  Of that cold, bitter, bleak December;
Though winter's sky was overcast,
  Though dull and dismal was the weather,
Snowflake and I—those times are past—
  Danced, sang, and whispered oft together!

II.

I called her Snowflake ; she looked bright
  As snow fresh fallen in the morning,
Just flushed by kiss of rosy light,
  Of sunny rays when day is dawning :
Her bosom mocked the snowdrops white
  That decked the tresses of my goddess ;
A truer heart or one more light
  Ne'er beat beneath a maiden's bodice.

III.

Ah, me ! I recollect those hours—
  Since then I've grown a trifle older—
I found just now some faded flow'rs,
  Reminding me of all I told her.
And Snowflake ?   Well, 'tis rather hard
  For hearts with one another smitten—
But, let me see, I think some bard
  Says "Lovers' vows in snow are written !"

K

A COVENT GARDEN CANTICLE.

I.

PINK blossoms fall and shatter
  Before the balmy breeze;
The rain has ceased to patter
  On newly-leafen trees;
The squares are green and shady,
  The parks are bright and gay—
Comes like a dainty lady,
  Sweet-scented, rosy May!

II.

Her home in Covent Garden
    Its glories I would vaunt—
I'm sure I beg her pardon,
    I mean her London haunt—
The brightest of all bowers,
    With dainty perfumes faint,
Decked out with sweetest flowers,
    Miss Mutrie loves to paint.

III.

Of crisp and cooling salads
    A Sybarite might sing ;
Or write enchanting ballads
    Of dishes for a king :
Amidst the banquet floral,
    He lazily might dream ;
And chant a pæan choral,
    On strawberries-and-cream

IV.

Sweet ruddy-cheeked Pomona
  Here, out of season, trips—
Of course we all have known her,
  With strawb'ry-stainëd lips.
Her freshness filched from peaches,
  Her tawny hair from pines,
Her voice which sweetly teaches
  Sweet lessons from the vines.

V.

In this town-house of Flora
  Where maids love time to kill;
Comes dainty, dimpled Dora,
  And laughter-loving Lil!
Come pets for bouquets longing,
  From Johnston's or from Buck's,
Round early green peas thronging—
  Delicious little ducks!

VI.

Sweet girls with eyes outvying

   The peerless gentian blue ;

Whose blushing cheeks are trying

   To rival peachen hue.

Each way a damsel goes is

   A sunbeam 'midst the gloom ;

And maidens mock the roses

   In rhapsody of bloom !

VII.

A bouquet for Ophelia

   When she appears to-night ;

The snowiest camelia

   For bridal bosom white.

A blushing blossom, paling

   'Fore cheeks of maidens gay—

Its charm is unavailing

   Near sweetest flowers of May !

VIII.

As pinkest petals perish,
  As brightest blossoms fade,
So droops the pet we cherish,
  So wanes each merry maid.
But glory sempiternal,
  Of sunshine loves to play,
When, lulled by breezes vernal,
  Bloom bonny flowers of May!

THE IMPARTIAL.

A Boat-Race Sketch.

I.

IN sorrow and joy she has seen the beginning—
　　Her lightness of spirit half dashed by the
　　　'blues'—
　　With cheers in her heart for the crew who are
　　　winning,
　　　While tears fill her eyes for those fated to lose.

II.

If you'll narrowly watch, 'mid the noise and conten-
　　tion,
　　You'll note, as her Arab paws proudly the dust,
A deftly-twined bouquet of speedwell and gentian
　　Beneath her white collar half carelessly thrust !

III.

The tint of a night in the still summer weather
   Her tight-fitting habit just serves to unfold,
While delicate cuffs are scarce fastened together
   By dainty-wrought fetters of turquoise and gold.

IV.

Ah, climax of sweet girlish neutral devices!
   What smiles for the winners, for losers what sighs!—
She has twined her fair hair with the colours of Isis,
   While those of the Cam glitter bright in her eyes.

TEN AND TWENTY.

A Drawing-Room Reverie.

I.

CAN ten long years have passed away
    Since with that baby Clarry Fay
        My boyish heart was smitten?
She was a charming little tease,
Who tore her clothes and grazed her knees,
Who sometimes clomb up apple-trees
        As agile as a kitten!

II.

The merriest of romping girls
Was Clarry, with her tangled curls;
　　　　All day her voice was trilling!
As, dancing madly to and fro,
Her full short skirt just served to show
Tucked trousers, white as driven snow—
　　　　A miracle of frilling.

III.

Whole mornings then were passed, I ween,
In paying homage to this queen
　　　　Of bread-and-butter misses;
Sometimes, when no one else was by,
I used to kiss her on the sly;
And Clarry was by no means shy,
　　　　But paid my kiss with kisses!

IV.

The livelong day we played and walked,

Or in the orchard swung and talked—

    'Twas thus our liking strengthened :

At last one gloomy, tearful day

My playfellow was sent away

To school, and there she had to stay—

    Until her frocks were lengthened.

V.

At Eton then in classic lore

I plunged, but liked the plunging more

    At 'Athens' with a shiver :

Both love and learning met their fate

When pulling in the College Eight ;

I quite forgot my little mate,

    When sculling on the river !

VI.

And now I met once more to-day
Not saucy Clare, but fair Miss Fay—
   The sweetest ' sweet and twenty!'
Who rules the season, for I know
At Prince's, Park, or flower-show,
In Opera-box, or in the Row,
   Her lovers throng in plenty.

VII.

Ah ! since that rosy, laughing child,
Would jump upon her pony wild
   And round the paddock canter ;
Or madly with black Hector race,
Or climb for nests in Lyndith Chase,
For which she got in sad disgrace,
   O tempora mutantur !

VIII.

Miss Fay will never know me now,

But with a studied, solemn bow

   She'll mask sweet dimpled Clarry—

Not know me? How her eyes flash bright!

She shakes my hand and grasps it tight!

And laughingly exclaims, "I'm right,

   'Tis my old playmate Harry!"

GEORGIE'S GIRDLE.

AH ! your supple slender waist
    Should be never tightly laced,
So leave each Nature's charm, sweet—
      As you found it :

If you want a tighter zone,
Some day, darling, when alone,
I'll wind a loving arm, sweet—
      Around it !

IN THE FOAM.

I.

COME where bright beauty unlooses her tresses,
  And emerald ripples scarce ruffle the sand !
Where mermaidens dance in the loveliest dresses,
  And white little feêt gaily sport on the strand !
Just watch the fair girls in their gambols capricious—
  No surf in the sunshine more fully at home—
See dimpled young darlings divinely delicious
  Bound over the breaker and flirt with the foam !

II.

In turquoise-hued trousers a fair Aphrodite—
    The rarest of rosy-cheeked plump little pets—
Hand in hand with a sweet little kissable Clytie,
    Distractingly dripping in pink pantalettes.
How dainty white limbs gaily flash in the billow !
    How musical voices sing over the sea !
While gracefully floating, with wave for a pillow,
    They gladden the shore with their resonant glee !

III.

O say then, stern cynic, with manner monastic,
    Wilt wander unmoved by our surf-beaten sands ?
When sweet summer sirens hold revel fantastic,
    And weave coloured weeds round their white little
        hands ?

They shake the salt spray in a torrent prismatic,

    They pout o'er the pebbles and swim o'er the

        shells ;

As light-hearted laughter grows yet more ecstatic,

    They dive where the queen of the mermaiden

        dwells !

IV.

Then fling back your hair from your sweet sunny

    faces,

    And ripple your locks to your delicate knees ;

While free from the fetters of latchets and laces,

    While sporting in sunshine and breasting the

        breeze !

Serene as the seagull so sleepily swaying,

    They fitfully flutter and restlessly roam :

These winsome young witches so prettily playing

    As brave as the breaker, as free as the foam.

L

COULEUR DE ROSE.

𝔄 𝔖𝔦𝔵 𝔐𝔬𝔫𝔱𝔥𝔰' 𝔊𝔬𝔲𝔯𝔱𝔰𝔥𝔦𝔭.

I.

ER soft sables, you must know,

    Kept off winter's frost and snow,

And the cruel wind did blow

    When we met :

The demurest little nun,

Though she'd sometimes change in fun,

Like a snowflake in the sun,—

    Little pet !

II.

Pray what meant those frequent sighs,

When those fathomless brown eyes

Sometimes gazed with glad surprise

Into mine ?

It was joy to be alone,

With my arm around her zone,

And to claim her for my own

Valentine !

III.

'For the romping wind of March

Was she bending like a larch,

As her glance seemed yet more arch

Through her curls :

Came in view the ankles neat,

Were revealed the dainty feet,

And the *chaussure* of my sweet

Girl of girls !

IV.

Ah ! my brightest fay of fays
Was most fickle in her ways,
In chameleon April days—
Sun and rain !
She would sometimes be put out,
She would laugh or cry and pout ;
Smiling through her tears in doubt,
Joy and pain !

V.

But in May so freshly fair
She would cull its blossoms rare,
Just to twine them in her hair—
Gay and wild :
A sweet pæan of perfume,
A gay sunny song of bloom,
She would chase away all gloom—
Laughing child !

VI.

In the balmy summer time,

With gay roses in their prime,

No one deems it is a crime

    Then to ' spoon ' !

So *sub rosá* 'neath bright bow'rs,

Over-heard by blushing flow'rs,

Did I whisper through sweet hours

    Once in June !

VII.

Ah ! her cheek will shame the rose,

With the tint that comes and goes,

And more radiantly glows,

    When it's prest !

Whilst her loving eyes flash bright,

With a sweet and sparkling light,

And white roses scarce look white

    In her breast !

VIII.

As the bee booms round the bed,

Where the petals pink are shed,

Sweetest honey from the red

  Softly sips :

So in moments half divine,

In sweet rapture I entwine

A slim waist whilst stealing mine—

  From her lips !

IX.

O ! when summer skies were blue,

And we fancied hearts were true,

While the long day loving through—

  Who'd suppose ?

Our grand castles built in Spain,

Or that love could ever wane,

And its fragrance but remain,

  Like the rose ?

AMANTIUM IRÆ.

I.

AM I forgiven?   You smile through your tears,
        love;
    May I return to your favour again?
Tell me, O quickly, and quiet my fears, love—
    Yours be the task, dear, to lighten my pain;
No more wet lashes, nor sobbing and pouting,
    Feelings of anger can't dwell in your breast—
Banish all sadness, all sorrow and doubting,
    Try to forget, when my fault is confest.
Grieved beyond measure, O say that I'm shriven,
Tell me, my treasure, now—Am I forgiven?

II.

Am I forgiven? Now dry your eyes, dearest,
　　You'd ne'er be hurt by Kate Calloner's wiles,
Look in my face now, your kindest and clearest,
　　Dimples look better, love, brimming with smiles :
Where was the harm in that least bit of flirting?
　　Chatting with Kate as she sat on the stair—
Could you imagine I meant to be hurting,
　　Trifling, or trying to cause you a care?
Man is but mortal, and hard have I striven,
Tell me, my pretty one—Am I forgiven?

III.

Am I forgiven? A sin one confesses,
　　Surely, my darling, is almost atoned—
Pitying glances and tender caresses,
　　Show me already my fault is condoned :

Sunshine at last, and of tears no more traces,

   Sweet smiles are striving to drive away sighs,

Pleasure o'erflushes the fairest of faces,

   Love is aglow in the brightest of eyes !

Faith nursed by charity ever has thriven—

What do you say, darling ?—Am I forgiven ?

A BREEZY BALLAD.

I.

OLD March flings golden tresses
  Over faces soft and sweet,
 And romps with skirts and dresses,
  Showing pretty legs and feet :
Each dimpled darling flushes,
 Looking coyly arch and fair,
With wealth of blooming blushes,
 Seen through tangled mass of hair !

II.

He comes down in a bustle
  From the mountains and the hills—
Makes sheeny skirts to rustle
  When revealing snowy frills.
He'll ruffle each gay feather,
  On these dainty little ducks—
Show boots of untanned leather
  'Neath their petticoats in tucks !

III.

Your nerves he may be shocking,
  When, some breezy afternoon,
He shows a silken stocking
  Or some silver-buckled shoon :
And p'r'aps you may be able,
  'Mid the surging broidered clothes,
To see boots edged with sable,
  With some quaintly-stripen hose.

IV.

O'er sealskin smooth he passes,
   And will make its surface rough ;
He'll chap red lips of lasses,
   And he'll knot a monkey muff :
But bright eyes still beam brighter—
   While each beauty looks more arch—
Light spirits yet grow lighter,
   'Neath the bracing breeze of March !

TANGLE LOCK.

𝔄 𝔖𝔨𝔢𝔱𝔠𝔥𝔢𝔯'𝔰 𝔖𝔬𝔫𝔤.

I.

AH! a rare old Lock was Tangle; you could
    sketch there or could angle,
    You could dream or moon or meditate all
      through the summer hours;
With its lime-trees all a-quiver, by the swiftly-flowing
    river,
    With its vines and grateful greenery, its beehives
    and its bowers.

II.

'Twas a miniature collection of rare pictures in perfection,

'Twas the rarest combination of bright flowers,
fruit, and trees;

There were honeysuckles tender, there were roses in
their splendour,

And hollyhocks of every tint scarce nodding in the
breeze.

III.

That quaint sunny porch rose-laden, and the soft-
eyed trustful maiden,

With the tangled briar dipping in the tuneful
brawling brook;

And the elms grand shadows flinging, with the grave
old rooks there swinging,

Were, I thought, the sort of pictures to be painted
in my book.

IV.

'Neath the limes so cool and shady, came a gentle
little lady,

Very often in the morning to our pleasant sketch-
ing-place;

In the daintiest of dresses, and sweet freshly-braided
tresses,

With a rosebud in her bosom and a smile upon
her face!

V.

She was young and fair and simple, and on either
cheek a dimple

Seemed to ask for lover's kisses, and her Christian
name was Kate;

Her grey eyes were soft and tender, and her figure
lithe and slender,

And her lips were round and ruddy, while her years
scarce doubled eight!

VI.

While the solemn rooks were cawing, she would slyly
watch me drawing,
And I'd try to read the meaning of those eloquent
grey eyes ;
In their undefined expression, did I find a mute confession,
Which half justified their drooping, and accounted
for her sighs.

VII.

'Twas thus I saw and drew her, and I thus began to
woo her,
To the humming of the dragon-fly and murmur of
the stream ;
Might I really then caress her?   Could I venture
then to press her
Little hand, or was I sleeping through a lovely
summer dream?

VIII.

If you'd listen to my story, I would tell you of the
glory,

Of the laziness and languor of those sleepy summer
days:

I could tell of woodland roaming and soft whispers
in the gloaming,

Of the laughter and the love-making and lotos-
eating laze!

IX.

I could tell of ballad-singing, and a sweet voice
clearly ringing,

To the queer old square piano in the quaint old-
fashioned room;

Of those silent moments golden, of a dainty waist
enfolden,

While the sweet grey eyes of Katie gladly glittered
in the gloom!

M

x.

P'r'aps my taste for art diminished, for my picture
ne'er was finished—

Though I made of Kate a study long before I did
depart,

Which I gave unto her father, for myself reserving
rather

The sweet study of a trustful and a loving little
heart !

LOVE-LOCKS.

I.

IN Arcady's fair groves there dwells
A Wizard, and 'tis there he sells
   All sorts of cunning beauty spells,
      From snow-white skins to blushes :
For pretty girls are scented toys ;
Young men can buy *pomade Hongroise ;*
There's hair-dye for the gay old boys,
      And ivory-backed brushes.

II.

There beauty's tresses are unfurled,
There blonde moustachios are twirled,
And darlings who have curls are curled,
  While those who've none buy plenty:
The Wizard keeps the key, 'tis true,
To turn grey locks to raven hue,
And makes bald coots of sixty-two
  Become smart youths of twenty.

III.

My hair is getting thin, and so
To Arcady I sometimes go
In search of ' balm,' for you must know
  I hold ' *Dum spiro, spero :* '
Though washes of all sorts I've tried,
And countless ointments have applied,
Old Time has made my parting wide,
  And sunk my hopes to zero.

IV.

The other day it came to pass,

I sat me down before the glass,

And saw reflected there, alas !

    A face grown old and jaded :

That face was scored by lines of care,

The forehead was quite high and bare ;

For, strange to say, the thick brown hair

    Of other days had faded !

V.

Ah, how that face has changed since times

Long passed away, when at 'The Limes'

My laughter rang with midnight chimes—

    My song was gay and early !

Then hearts were hearts, and blue were skies,

And tender were sweet Lucy's eyes—

When I believed in woman's sighs,

    My locks were thick and curly !

VI.

As Mr. Wizard snips and snips,

I think of Lucy's laughing lips,

And whilst he just takes off the tips,

    I muse on bygone pleasures:

At home I have a tiny tress

Of soft brown hair; I must confess,

Although it caused me much distress,

    'Tis treasured 'mid my treasures.

VII.

Ah, would that night come back again

When she took from her *châtelaine*

Her scissors!—it was not in vain.

    I hear her laugh the while her

Fingers, dimpled soft and fair,

Thrill as she clips one lock of hair;

While I, like Samson, sit still there,

    And smile on sweet Dalilah.

VIII.

When blonde and brown locks interlace,
Or scented tresses sweep your face,
While laughter unto sighs gives place,
    And pouting lips are present ;
Or meek grey eyes droop still more meek,
And dimples play at hide-and-seek,
There's but one language lips can speak—
    'Tis brief, but rather pleasant !

IX.

In place of Lucy's hand I feel
The chilly touch of Wizard's steel,
Who brings me back from the ideal,
    By talk of lime-juice water ;
And beauty's fingers no more hold
My locks—they're by the barber sold
To stuff arm-chairs ; sometimes, I'm told,
    They're used to mix with mortar !

X.

And Lucy? She's at Bangalore,
And married to old Colonel Bore ;
They say she flirts from two to four—

    Indeed, I do not doubt them.

'Tis hard to steer among the rocks
Of life, without some awkward knocks ;
They say that 'Love laughs loud at locks'—

    He howls at those without them !

THE KING OF THE CRADLE.

A Baby Idyll.

I.

RAW back the cradle-curtains, Kate,
　　While watch and ward you're keeping,
Let's see the monarch in his state,
　　And view him whilst he's sleeping.

He smiles and clasps his tiny hand,
　With sunbeams o'er him gleaming—
A world of baby fairyland
　He visits while he's dreaming.

II.

Monarch of pearly powder-puff
　Asleep in nest so cosy,
Shielded from breath of breezes rough
　By curtains warm and rosy :
He slumbers soundly in his cell,
　As weak as one decrepid,
Though King of Coral, Lord of Bell,
　And Knight of Bath that's tepid !

III.

Ah, lucky tyrant !　Happy lot !
　Fair watchers without number,
Who sweetly sing beside his cot,
　And hush him off to slumber ;
White hands in wait to smooth so neat
　His pillow when it's rumpled—
A couch of rose leaves soft and sweet,
　Not one of which is crumpled !

IV.

Will yonder dainty, dimpled hand—

    Size, nothing and a quarter—

E'er grasp a sabre, lead a band,

    To glory and to slaughter?

Or, may I ask, will those blue eyes—

    In baby *patois* 'peepers'—

E'er in the House of Commons rise,

    And strive to catch the Speaker's?

V.

Will that smooth brow o'er Hansard frown,

    Confused by lore statistic?

Or will those lips e'er stir the town

    From pulpit ritualistic?

Will e'er that tiny Sybarite

    Become an author noted?

That little brain the world's delight,

    Its work by all men quoted?

VI.

Though rosy, dimpled, plump, and round,
  Though fragile, soft, and tender,
Sometimes, alas ! it may be found
  The thread of life is slender !
A little shoe, a bitten glove—
  Affection never waning—
The shattered idol of our love
  Is all that is remaining !

VII.

Then does one chance, in fancy, hear
  . Small feet in childish patter,
Tread soft as they a grave draw near,
  And voices hush their chatter ;
'Tis small and new ; they pause in fear,
  Beneath the grey church tower,
To consecrate it by a tear
  And deck it with a flower.

VIII.

Who can predict the future, Kate—

 Your fondest aspiration !

Who knows the solemn laws of fate,

 That govern our creation ?

Who knows what lot awaits your boy—

 Of happiness or sorrow ?

Sufficient for to-day is joy,

 Leave tears, sweet, for to-morrow !

A LITTLE LOVE-LETTER.

I.

PRETTY pet with the tangled hair,

    Going to muse by the summer sea—

O dimpled darling with cheeks so fair,

Tell me, O dearest, when musing there,

    Will you think of me?

II.

O sweetest sweet, when the salt breeze sighs

    'Mid silken locks ever flowing free,

While gulls glint white against sleepy skies,

Will looks of those bright brown loving eyes

    E'er be turned to me?

III.

Ah, laughing child, when your eyes beam bright,

And lips are parted in girlish glee ;

When the shore is glad in still summer night,

With your sweet soft smile, and your laughter light,

Do you smile on me ?

IV.

When the moon is up, and sleeps the land

To tender music in minor key ;

When the silver-ripples hush the strand

And scarcely dimple the golden sand,

Will you dream of me ?

V.

Poor little heart ! when your cheeks are wet

With tears that sadden one's heart to see,

Your moist lips tremble—you can't forget

Sometimes the sun through the rain shines, pet,

When you weep for me !

TWO CHRISTMAS EVES.

I.

WITHOUT, the trees are swerving,
  With wild, uncertain curving—
For the wind is howling sadly, and all is dull and
    drear.
  Whilst listening to its moaning,
  Its sighing and its groaning,
Comes back to me the memory of many a bygone
    year !

II.

Within, are merry faces,

Glad with a thousand graces ;

Whilst berries red mock maiden lips 'midst loving

mistletoe !

As bright eyes flash the brighter,

And every heart grows lighter—

Beneath the cheery influence of Christmas' ruddy

glow.

III.

When snowflakes down are floating,

Whilst a weird and rimy coating

Weaves its mystic, lace-like pattern all o'er the win-

dow-pane ;

E'en when the fire burns brightest,

E'en when the laugh is lightest,

I mind me of those dear old times ne'er to come back

again !

N

IV.

That silvery laughter ringing

Sad memory is bringing,

That Christmas-time was once to me as merry and as

gay—

Now every smile and gladness

Is mingled with a sadness,

Of pledges made — since broken — on that dull

December day !

V.

How well can I remember

That drear day in December !

We whispered in yon curtained bay, in accents low

and few :

A soft white hand I pressed there,

Whilst a trembling voice confessed there,

Words of love so lovingly that I'd fain believe them

true !

VI.

, That that sweet voice was lying,

'Twixt smiling and 'twixt sighing,

In the bitterest of anguish I will ne'er consent to

own ;

Yet no fond face is near me,

To smile upon or cheer me,

At Christmas, as in days agone.—I sit and muse

alone !

VII.

Can true love be more rare now,

Or beauty e'en less fair now,

And hearts composed of sterner stuff than those of

former times ?

For Christmas seems less cheery—

Indeed, bygone and weary—

Most unutterably dreary to him who pens these

rhymes !

VIII.

Thus often in the gloaming

My saddened thoughts are roaming—

Whilst winter winds are blowing, and the fire is burn-

ing low,

As I sit here and ponder,

My memory will wander

To hopes and joys of Christmas on that night of long

ago.

MOTHER O' PEARL.

I.

 PEARL is the sweetest creation
　　E'er shod with the tiniest boots—
I wish she had ne'er a relation,
　　I wish I'd a balance with Coutts!
They say Pearl is so like her mother;
　Was she like my pet when a girl?
Will pet become just such another,
　Some day as the Mother o' Pearl?

II.

My Pearl is the prettiest kitten,
    She laughs—will she ever grow fat?
Or e'er, with mad jealousy smitten,
    Develop the mind of a cat?
Her figure get round as a bubble?
    Her hair lose its exquisite curl?
Her chin get undimpled and double,
    Like that of the Mother o' Pearl?

III.

Will Pearl become pert and capricious,
    And haughty and give herself airs?
(I thought, when she looked so delicious
    Last night when we sat on the stairs.)
Will she patronise *me* in her bounty,
    And boast of her uncle the Earl?
Or talk with cold pride of the county,
    As often does Mother o' Pearl?

IV.

Will Pearl ever sneer at her betters,

   Or e'er act the amateur spy?

And try to read other folk's letters,

   Or listen at doors on the sly? . . .

If boy to the man be the father,

   Mama to the woman is—girl—-

As daughter-in-law I would rather

   Not father the Mother o' Pearl!

HER NEST.

I.

LIKE the tiny pet of a sculptor's dream,
    Half smothered in delicate trifle cream,
    Like Aphrodite in sea-foam tost,
Or a lovely girl in a snow-drift lost :
With her dimpled hand to her red lips prest,
She smiles as she sleeps in her warm white nest.
    She sleeps, as a sunbeam through curtain creeps,
    And a soft white bosom 'neath cambric peeps,
                She sleeps.

II.

Her lissome figure 'tis hard to trace

'Neath the snowy linen and filmy lace ;

With her chesnut hair o'er the pillow spread,

Like an aureola around her head ;

A sweet living saint on Carrara tomb,

She smiles as she dreams in her dainty room.

    She dreams in her sleep of the sunny beams

    That dare kiss her cheek with their rosy gleams—

            She dreams !

IN THE GRAPERY.

I.

THICK hang the peaches one gathers so readily—
 Shrunken the stream running down to the
  sea—
Plums on the wall ripen slowly and steadily,
 To song of the reaper low hummeth the bee.
Sultry's the sunshine so hot in the pinery,
 Orange and russet are tinting the leaves,
Luscious ripe clusters bloom black in the vinery,
 Yellow the meadows with golden-eared sheaves.

II.

Heat of the noontide is rising there hazily—

  Culling bright flowers their hair to entwine,

Light-hearted lasses are lounging there lazily,

  Plucking the purple that hangs from the vine,

Singing and laughing in fulness of pleasure there,

  Roving at random and choosing by chance,

Piling up pictures of glowing rich treasure there,

  Worthy the pencil of Duffield or Lance.

III.

Ruddy-bloomed clusters are getting importunate,

  Fain to be martyred along with the rest;

Weep as they gaze on and envy the fortunate

  Rosebud asleep on my lady-love's breast!

Would that my change unto grapes were permissible!

  Lovingly toying, I'd kiss and ne'er tell—

Pressed close to lips so delightfully kissable,

  Ripe ruby lips of my sweet little Nell!

A NUTSHELL NOVEL.

For a Miniature Mudie.

VOL. I.

 WINNING wile,
A sunny smile,
A feather:
A tiny talk,
A pleasant walk,
Together!

VOL. II.

A little doubt,

A playful pout,

    Capricious :

A merry miss,

A stolen kiss,

    Delicious ! !

VOL. III.

You ask mama,

Consult papa,

    With pleasure :

And both repent,

This rash event,

    At leisure ! ! !

A Gallery of Girls.

"Six girls who are now staying at the Hall are so typical of
the pictures of six well-known artists, that they are now always
called by the names of the painters instead of their own."—
Extract from a letter from the country.

I.

MISS LIZZIE LESLIE.

 WHO can paint the picture of my pet?
      As 'mid the grey-green hay she child-like
            kneels,
  Who shows a dainty slipper, then conceals
'Neath tangled grass its celadon rosette.
A soft white robe, a broidered chemisette
    Scarce veils her rounded bosom, as it steals
    A subtle charm from that it half reveals—
As sweet and modest as the violet!

A gipsy hat casts shadows, pearly grey,

    Across the golden sunshine of her smile.

Her glance e'en cynics dare not disobey,

    Her dimples even iron hearts beguile—

A dainty despot on a throne of hay,

    Who conquers all by magic girlish wile !

II.

MISS PEPITA PHILLIP.

 BEAUTY from the sunny South I crown
With this unworthy laurel of my lay.
Her glossy raven tresses, notice pray,
From which a lace mantilla ripples down,
To half conceal her lip-red silken gown.
Note burning eyes, which flash from grave to gay,
And cheeks so kissed by ardent sunny ray,
That bright carnation blushes through the brown!

No baby kiss-play lurks in *that* ripe mouth,

    Nor trifling with effete coquettish art ;

But earnest passion of the sunny South—

    To love or die, with all its soul and heart !

If *she* should hate to love, how sad your fate ;

But sadder still if she should love to hate !

III.

MISS GERTIE GAINSBOROUGH.

AH ! thrice happy the crumpled red rose leaves,
    Asleep on her bosom so warm and white ;
  And the turquoise ribbon half lost to sight,
In the silken tresses it interweaves !
Thrice happy the mortal who once receives,
    From her fathomless eyes so brown and bright,
    The radiant glances of inner light
That glitter from under their drooping eaves.

Ah! sweet are those eloquent lips a-pout,

    Whose pleadings a stoic could scarce resist,

Now rounded in rapture, now drooped in doubt,

    But daintily red as if newly kist.

'Tis joy to believe in the truth that lies

Far down in the depths of those sweet brown eyes!

IV.

MISS MINNIE MILLAIS.

'MID falling blossoms dreams my lady fair—
 What lustrous splendour in those deep
        blue eyes,
    That half reflect the tint of southern skies !
What gold-lit glory in that chesnut hair,
Down rippling on her dimpled shoulders bare !
    What poet's song could half her charms comprise,
    Or painter's brush her grace immortalize ?—
So sweet, so queenly, and so debonair.

'Mid falling blossoms, pink and ruby red

    My lady strolls with calm majestic mien,

Though lips are mocked by roses overhead,

    And cheeks by shattered damask on the green,

And bosom by the fairest Guelder shed—

    She reigns of all the roses still the queen !

V.

MISS ROSIE LEECH.

DOWN on the sands there strolls a merry maid,
  Aglow with ruddy health and gladsome glee;
She breasts the breezes of the summer sea,
And lets each zephyr trifle with each braid;
Laughs gaily as her petticoats evade
  Her girlish grasp and wildly flutter free,
  As, bending to some boisterous decree,
The neatest foot and ankle are displayed.

Her youthful rounded figure you may trace

    Half pouting, as rude Boreas unfurls

A wealth of snowy frillery and lace,

    A glory of soft golden rippled curls.

Comes, blushing with a rare unconscious grace,

    The bonniest of England's bonny girls !

VI.

MISS CECIL SANDYS.

SEE how she crouches on an autumn morn,
    Where poppies 'mid the corn play hide-and-
        seek,
  And plucks them in an idle girlish freak.
Her lips are curved with ill-disguisëd scorn,
Her tresses wear the tint of sunburnt corn ;
  And poppies might have stained her flaming cheek :
  A modern maiden, with a grace antique—
A dainty damsel, lovely and lovelorn !

Proud as beautiful, passionate as proud,

    She twists and bites her tawny, tangled mane ;

While eyes the tint of purple thunder-cloud

    Flash fiercely with an eloquent disdain !

And then that haughty head is bowed—

    A song of sorrow and a poem of pain.

DEDICATION.

O, SOME-ONE, if your laughing eyes,
Beam brighter with a glad surprise,
  I know by intuition,
You'll deign to look this volume through,
I dedicate, my sweet, to you,
  Without your ' kind permission.'

Ah! will it make you frown and pout?
Or will you think, beyond all doubt,
  No better muse than mine is?
And will you laugh, or sigh and weep?
Or will you, darling, go to sleep
  Before you get to

  FINIS ?

THE TEMPLE, *September 1876.*

EXTRACTS FROM OPINIONS OF THE PRESS

ON

BOUDOIR BALLADS,

BY

J. ASHBY-STERRY.

Land and Water.

'One of the most charming books that we have come across for a long time. From cover to cover there is not a single dull page in it. Mr. Sterry's book is the fruit of a healthy, happy mind, of the experience of a man who is willing to see that men are still honest, women good and pure. . . . The whole book, in its unaffectedly poetic tone, genial humour, and remarkable finish of style, is quite one of the very best books of the year.'

Home News.

'A volume of verse excellent in its light and sportive way, and certain to be popular with a very wide circle of readers.'

Nonconformist.

'We cannot say that we feel that we have done full justice to Mr. Sterry's delightful volume, for the best of the pieces are too long for us to quote *in extenso*. . . . We have no doubt that by a large circle of readers this book will be eagerly welcomed, and furnish a new source of innocent pleasure to not a few.'

Pictorial World.

'Mr. Sterry has long been known as one of the happiest of versifiers, and to read his songs is something like enjoying a feast of strawberries and cream in the best of all good company. . . . "Boudoir Ballads" is emphatically a volume that every lover of light and graceful poetry should possess, as being a book to be turned to and read again and again.'

Morning Post.

'Enchanting ballads. . . . It is not possible to dwell on the elaborate beauty of the metrical forms here adopted, but we cannot part from this delightful volume without a word of praise on the score of the writer's easy, elegant, and melodious measures, than which he could have chosen no more charming or more effective vehicle for these latest, and we trust not the last, inspirations of his muse.'

Observer.

'Mr. Sterry is a delightful companion; at his best he is well-nigh without a rival amongst light-hearted songsters. . . . His *vers de société* are altogether admirable of their kind; and the dainty task upon which he has expended his labour of love could not possibly be accomplished with more winning grace of manner, or more genial melody of expression.'

Court Journal.

'A volume of charming verses full of graceful fancy. No more appropriate title could have been given to these fascinating *vers de société.*'

Notes and Queries.

'Mr. Sterry is a master in drawing-room verses. . . . His nymphs with pretty adornings are not exactly made for the wear and tear of life, but they are pretty things for a swain to sing in graceful roundelettes. Mr. Sterry's book will have to stand the wear and tear of a world of readers. When they have got through it they will find themselves refreshed and invigorated, and that is no little testimony in its favour.'

Leeds Mercury.

'Apt in every way is the title Mr. Sterry has bestowed upon his collection of society verses. The volume itself is one of the daintiest that has yet been published. With its softly-toned paper, artistic embellishments, and dainty binding, it is just the book for Beauty to lay upon her private table, and to open in her moments of luxurious weariness or *ennui*. Wholly in keeping with the appearance are the contents. Before all living competitors Mr. Sterry is the poet of society as it now exists.

Wherever pretty girls may be expected, there their bard is to be found. Gaily and a trifle saucily he sings of them, their desires and their doings. . . . He carols joyously and well.'

Weekly Times.

'He seems to have the power of touching with his magic talisman the most commonplace objects, and transmuting them into gold.'

Glasgow News of the Week.

'This truly is a tome which the delicate hands of Beauty will hold fondly as the lustrous eyes glance rapidly over the fascinating pages; for is not this, so to speak, the epic of British girlhood? . . . Mr. Sterry sings but as the linnet sings, and with no language but a delightful chirrup, which sounds throughout his pages. Graceful fancy is the key-note of his work, as becomes the general subject of his song.'

Bell's Weekly Messenger.

'This very pleasant volume of genuine verse. . . . There is a smoothness about the rhythm of the contents of this volume which is most gratifying, and an absence of striving after meretricious effects which it is delightful to meet with.'

Bell's Life in London.

'The verses might have been printed on rose leaves, with ink made from the ebon juices distilled from a bee's treasury of hidden sweets. There is, however, no lack of a Puck-like humour in this very charming collection of "Boudoir Ballads." Certain portions of Mr. Sterry's verses remind us of the quaint quatrains of Théophile Gautier and the tender utterances of Alfred de Musset; they are so replete with refined sentiment and that perfect ease which springs from a cultivation of the minstrelsy of elegant thoughts and harmonious ideas, known only to the lovers of gentle and habitual nature. . . . A fascinating book of exquisite niceness.'

Glasgow Evening News.

'Of our maidens Mr. Sterry sings more delightfully, perhaps, than any other living master of what may be called the drawing-room lyre. . . . "Boudoir Ballads" forms one of the best possible gifts that could be offered by lover to his lady, and should, besides, be read by everybody who delights in bright and brief verse.'

Yorkshire Post.

'The book abounds with pretty thoughts delightfully expressed. . . . Although there is now and again a strain in the minor key, there is so much sunshine and good spirits about the volume, that it is quite infectious, and it will help to while away many an otherwise sad hour in the coming dark days of winter.'

Derbyshire Times.

'Mr. Sterry's style is enchantingly graceful. Each of his poems exhibits delicacy of diction, refinement of touch, playfulness of fancy, sly humour, arrowy wit, and quaintness of conceit. We shall be disappointed if "Boudoir Ballads" do not supply the sensation of the season.'

Vanity Fair.

'Ballads which, though dedicated to the boudoir, are not altogether unworthy of the more sedate library.'

Liverpool Albion.

'There is a light, healthy playfulness about his work which is sure to please, while he never descends into burlesque, or offends by treating a really serious subject in a trifling manner.'

Saunders's News Letter.

'Mr. Sterry's verse is always polished, musical, and epigrammatic. When the next volume of collected *vers de société* appears, "Boudoir Ballads" must be freely represented.'

Hornet.

'This most fascinating volume. . . . Nothing more fascinating has appeared since Praed published his ever-famous volume. United in "Boudoir Ballads" will be found all the gifts, charms, and graces that go to the perfecting of the *vers de société*. . . . The whole work is the fruit of a gentle nature and of a well-balanced mind. . . . One of the most charming books that ever we have met with.'

CHATTO & WINDUS'S
LIST OF BOOKS.

NEW FINE-ART GIFT-BOOK, UNIFORM WITH THE
"TURNER GALLERY."

Handsomely half-bound, India Proofs, royal folio, £10 ; Large Paper
copies, Artists' India Proofs, elephant folio, £20.

M o d e r n   A r t:

A Series of superb Line Engravings, from the Works of distinguished
Painters of the English and Foreign Schools, selected from Galleries
and Private Collections in Great Britain.

With Descriptive Text by JAMES DAFFORNE.

Demy 8vo, price One Shilling.

Academy Notes for 1876.

With 107 Illustrations of the Principal Pictures at Burlington
House : a large number being Facsimiles of Sketches drawn by
the Artists. Edited by HENRY BLACKBURN.

"*We at once take an opportunity of offering our thanks, as well as those of all
visitors to the Exhibition, to Mr. Blackburn for his very carefully executed review
of the Academy pictures, illustrated by some* 100 *woodcut memoranda of the
principal pictures, almost half of them from the pencils of the painters themselves.
A cheaper, prettier, or more convenient souvenir of the Exhibition it would be
difficult to conceive and unreasonable to expect.*"—TIMES.

. ACADEMY NOTES *for* 1875 *may also be had, price One Shilling.*

Crown 8vo, with Coloured Frontispiece and Illustrations, cloth
gilt, 7s. 6d.

A History of Advertising.

From the Earliest Times. Illustrated by Anecdotes, Curious
Specimens, and Biographical Notes of Successful Advertisers.
By HENRY SAMPSON.

" We have here a book to be thankful for. Among the many interesting illustra-
tions is a photographed copy of the 'Times' for January 1st, 1788, which may be
easily read by means of a magnifying glass. We recommend the present volume,
which takes us through antiquity, the Middle Ages, and the present time, illustrat-
ing all in turn by advertisements—serious, comic, roguish, or downright rascally.
The chapter on 'swindles and hoaxes' is full of entertainment; but of that the
volume itself is full from the first page to the last."—ATHENÆUM.

Crown 4to, containing 24 Plates beautifully printed in Colours, with
descriptive Text, cloth extra, gilt, 6s.

Æsop's Fables

Translated into Human Nature.   By C. H. BENNETT.

" For fun and frolic the new version of Æsop's Fables must bear away the
palm. There are plenty of grown-up children who like to be amused; and if this
new version of old stories does not amuse them they must be very dull indeed,
and their situation one much to be commiserated."—MORNING POST.

Crown 8vo, with Portrait and Facsimile, cloth extra, 7s. 6d.

Artemus Ward's Works:

The Works of CHARLES FARRER BROWNE, better known as
ARTEMUS WARD.   With Portrait, facsimile of Handwriting, &c.

" The author combines the powers of Thackeray with those of Albert Smith.
The salt is rubbed in with a native hand—one which has the gift of tickling."—
SATURDAY REVIEW.

Small 4to, green and gold, 6s. 6d. ; gilt edges, 7s. 6d.

As Pretty as Seven,

and other Popular German Stories.   Collected by LUDWIG
BECHSTEIN.   With Additional Tales by the Brothers GRIMM,
and 100 Illustrations by RICHTER.

" These tales are pure and healthful; they will. heal over childhood a rosy
light, and strew the path with stars and flowers, the remembrance of which will
last through life."—PREFACE.

Blake's Works.

A Series of Reproductions in Facsimile of the Works of WILLIAM
BLAKE, including the "Songs of Innocence and Experience,"
"The Book of Thel," "America," "The Vision of the Daughters
of Albion," "The Marriage of Heaven and Hell," "Europe, a
Prophecy," "Jerusalem," "Milton," "Urizen," "The Song of
Los," &c.   *[In preparation.*

Demy 8vo, cloth extra, with Illustrations, 18s.

Baker's Clouds in the East :

Travels and Adventures on the Perso-Turkoman Frontier. By
VALENTINE BAKER. With Maps and Illustrations, coloured
and plain, from Original Sketches. Second Edition, revised and
corrected.

"*A man who not only thinks for himself, but who has risked his life in order to
gain information. . . . . A most graphic and lively narrative of travels and
adventures which have nothing of the commonplace about them.*"—LEEDS
MERCURY.

Crown 8vo, cloth extra, 7s. 6d.

A Handbook of London Bankers ;

With some Account of their Predecessors, the Early Goldsmiths ;
together with Lists of Bankers, from the Earliest London Directory, printed in 1677, to that of the London Post-Office Directory
of 1876. By F. G. HILTON PRICE.

"*An interesting and unpretending little work, which may prove a useful contribution towards the history of a difficult subject. . . . Mr. Price's anecdotes
are entertaining. . . . There is something fascinating, almost romantic,
in the details given us of Child's Bank. . . . There is a great deal of amusing
reading and some valuable information in this book.*"—SATURDAY REVIEW.

"*A work of considerable research and labour; an instructive contribution to
the history of the enormous wealth of the City of London.*"—ACADEMY.

Crown 8vo, cloth extra, 9s.

Bardsley's Our English Surnames :

Their Sources and Significations. By CHARLES WAREING
BARDSLEY, M.A. Second Edition, revised throughout, considerably enlarged, and partially rewritten.

"*Mr. Bardsley has faithfully consulted the original mediæval documents and
works from which the origin and development of surnames can alone be satisfac-
torily traced. He has furnished a valuable contribution to the literature of surnames, and we hope to hear more of him in this field.*"—TIMES.

Small 8vo, cloth extra, with Frontispiece by CRUIKSHANK, 3s. 6d.

Blewitt's The Rose and the Lily ;

How they became the Emblems of England and France. A Fairy
Tale. By Mrs. OCTAVIAN BLEWITT. With a Frontispiece by
GEORGE CRUIKSHANK.

Crown 8vo, cloth extra gilt, with Illustrations, 7s. 6d.

Boccaccio's Decameron ;

or, Ten Days' Entertainment. Translated into English, with an
Introduction by THOMAS WRIGHT, Esq., M.A., F.S.A. With
Portrait, and STOTHARD'S beautiful Copperplates.

B

Imperial 4to, cloth extra, gilt and gilt edges, price 21*s.* per volume.

Beautiful Pictures by British Artists :

A Gathering of Favourites from our Picture Galleries. · In Two Series.

The FIRST SERIES including Examples by WILKIE, CONSTABLE, TURNER, MULREADY, LANDSEER, MACLISE, E. M. WARD, FRITH, Sir JOHN GILBERT, LESLIE, ANSDELL, MARCUS STONE, Sir NOEL PATON, FAED, EYRE CROWE, GAVIN O'NEIL, and MADOX BROWN.

The SECOND SERIES containing Pictures by ARMYTAGE, FAED, GOODALL, HEMSLEY, HORSLEY, MARKS, NICHOLLS, Sir NOEL PATON, PICKERSGILL, G. SMITH, MARCUS STONE, SOLOMON, STRAIGHT, E. M. WARD, and WARREN.

All engraved on Steel in the highest style of Art. Edited, with Notices of the Artists, by SYDNEY ARMYTAGE, M.A.

Each Volume is Complete in itself.

" *This book is well got up, and good engravings by Jeens, Lumb Stocks, and others, bring back to us pictures of Royal Academy Exhibitions of past years.*" —TIMES.

Price One Shilling Monthly, with Four Illustrations.

Belgravia.

Contents of the November Number.—EXCHANGE OF ANIMALS. By CHARLES READE. Illustrated. ASTROLOGY. By RICHARD A. PROCTOR. JOSHUA HAGGARD'S DAUGHTER. By M. E. BRADDON. Illustrated. THE NEW REPUBLIC ; Culture, Faith, and Philosophy. LOST. Illustrated. AN AUNT BY MARRIAGE. By JAMES PAYN. FROM DREAMS TO WAKING. By E. L. LINTON. QUIPS AND CRANKS AT OUR CLUB WINDOW. JULIET. By Mrs. H. LOVETT CAMERON. Illustrated.

The THIRTIETH Volume of BELGRAVIA (which includes the HOLIDAY NUMBER), *elegantly bound in crimson cloth, bevelled boards, full gilt side and back, gilt edges, price 7s.6d., is now ready.—Cases for binding the volume (designed by Luke Limner) can be had at 2s. each.*

Price One Shilling, with numerous Illustrations,

The Belgravia Annual

for Christmas, 1876.

Contents.—THE CONFISCATED WEEDS. By JAMES PAYN. Illustrated by JOSEPH NASH. COMING EVENTS. Illustrated by E. WAGNER. CARMAGNOLE ; or, The Wickedest Woman in France. By GEORGE AUGUSTUS SALA. THE IMPROPER SPECTRE. With Illustrations by JAMES SULLIVAN. PLAIN JOHN SMITH. AT THE DOOR. Illustrated by LAURA BLOOD. MONSIEUR BLAISE. By DUTTON COOK. THE WOLF AND THE LAMB. Illustrated by AGNES FURNIVALL. THE ROCKING STONE OF TREGUNC. By KATHARINE S. MACQUOID. Illustrated by T. R. MACQUOID. HER LAST APPEARANCE. By M. E. BRADDON. THE OLD BELL-RINGER. By M. CECIL HAY. Illustrated by R. P. LEITCH. THE PARSON'S PUPIL. By S. J. MACKENNA. Illustrated by J. MAHONEY. NELLY O'HARA ; or, The Half-Brothers. THE LADIES VANE, SPINSTERS.

Crown 8vo, with Photographic Portrait, cloth extra, 9s.

Blanchard's (Laman) Poems.

Now first Collected. Edited, with a Life of the Author (including numerous hitherto unpublished Letters from Lord LYTTON, LAMB, DICKENS, ROBERT BROWNING, and others), by BLAN-CHARD JERROLD.

"*His humorous verse is much of it admirable—sparkling with genuine 'esprit,' and as polished and pointed as Praed's.*"—SCOTSMAN.

Crown 8vo, cloth extra, gilt, 6s.

Boudoir Ballads:

Vers de Société. By J. ASHBY-STERRY.

Crown 8vo, cloth extra, gilt, 7s. 6d.

Brand's Observations on Popular Anti-

quities, chiefly Illustrating the Origin of our Vulgar Customs, Ceremonies, and Superstitions. With the Additions of Sir HENRY ELLIS. An entirely New and Revised Edition, with fine full-page Illustrations.

"*Anyone who will read, on each respective day, the chapter which belongs to it, will, when he has got through the volume, have a better notion of what English history is than he will get from almost any other work professedly named a 'history.'*"—QUARTERLY REVIEW.

Crown 8vo, cloth extra, 7s. 6d.

Bret Harte's Select Works

in Prose and Poetry. With Introductory Essay by J. M. BEL-LEW, Portrait of the Author, and 50 Illustrations.

"*Not many months before my friend's death, he had sent me two sketches of a young American writer (Bret Harte), far away in California ('The Outcasts of Poker Flat,' and another), in which he had found such subtle strokes of character as he had not anywhere else in late years discovered; the manner resembling himself, but the matter fresh to a degree that had surprised him; the painting in all respects masterly, and the wild rude thing painted a quite wonderful reality. I have rarely known him more honestly moved.*"—FORSTER'S LIFE OF DICKENS.

Small crown 8vo, cloth extra, gilt, with full-page Portraits, 4s. 6d.

Brewster's (Sir David) Martyrs of

Science.

Small crown 8vo, cloth extra, gilt, with Astronomical Plates, 4s. 6d.

Brewster's (Sir David) More Worlds

than One, the Creed of the Philosopher and the Hope of the Christian.

Crown 8vo, cloth, full gilt (from a special and novel design), 10s. 6d.

The Bric-a-Brac Hunter;

or, Chapters on Chinamania. By Major H. BYNG HALL. With Photographic Frontispiece.

"This is a delightful book. His hints respecting marks, texture, finish, and character of various wares will be useful to amateurs. By all who are interested in Chinamania it will be most warmly appreciated—a very amusing and chatty volume."—STANDARD.

Small crown 8vo, cloth extra, 6s.

Brillat-Savarin's Gastronomy as a Fine

Art; or, The Science of Good Living. A Translation of the "Physiologie du Goût" of BRILLAT-SAVARIN, with an Introduction and Explanatory Notes by R. E. ANDERSON, M.A.

"I could write a better book of cookery than has ever yet been written; it should be a book on philosophical principles."—Dr. JOHNSON.

THE STÓTHARD BUNYAN.—Crown 8vo, cloth extra, gilt, 7s. 6d.

Bunyan's Pilgrim's Progress.

Edited by Rev. T. SCOTT. With 17 beautiful Steel Plates by STOTHARD, engraved by GOODALL; and numerous Woodcuts.

Crown 8vo, cloth extra, gilt, with Illustrations, 7s. 6d.

Byron's Letters and Journals.

With Notices of his Life. By THOMAS MOORE. A Reprint of the Original Edition, newly revised, Complete in one thick Volume, with Twelve full-page Plates.

"We have read this book with the greatest pleasure. Considered merely as a composition, it deserves to be classed among the best specimens of English prose which our age has produced. . . . The style is agreeable, clear, and manly, and, when it rises into eloquence, it rises without effort or ostentation. Nor is the matter inferior to the manner. It would be difficult to name a book which exhibits more kindness, fairness, and modesty."—MACAULAY.

Demy 4to, cloth extra, gilt edges, 31s. 6d.

Canova's Works in Sculpture and Model-

ling. 150 Plates, exquisitely engraved in Outline by MOSES, and printed on an India tint. With Descriptions by the Countess ALBRIZZI, a Biographical Memoir by CICOGNARA, and Portrait by WORTHINGTON.

"The fertility of this master's resources is amazing, and the manual labour expended on his works would have worn out many an ordinary workman. The outline engravings are finely executed. The descriptive notes are discriminating, and in the main exact."—SPECTATOR.

"A very handsome volume. . . . The graceful designs of the original are rendered by the engraver with exquisite fidelity. As a gift-book, the volume deserves to be placed beside the 'Outlines' of a very kindred genius—Flaxman."—GRAPHIC.

Small 4to, cloth gilt, with Coloured Illustrations, 10s. 6d.

Chaucer for Children :

A Golden Key. By Mrs. H. R. HAWEIS. With Eight Coloured
Pictures and numerous Woodcuts by the Author.

Two Vols. imperial 8vo, cloth extra, gilt, the Plates beautifully
printed in Colours, £3 3s.

Catlin's Illustrations of the Manners,

Customs, and Condition of the North American Indians : the result of Eight Years of Travel and Adventure among the Wildest
and most Remarkable Tribes now existing. Containing 360
Coloured Engravings from the Author's original Paintings.

Imperial folio, half-morocco, gilt, £7 10s.

Catlin's North American Indian Port-

folio : Hunting Scenes, Amusements, Scenery, and Costume of the
Indians of the Rocky Mountains and Prairies. A series of 31
magnificent Plates, coloured in facsimile of the Original Drawings.

Crown 8vo, cloth extra, gilt, 7s. 6d.

Colman's Humorous Works:

"Broad Grins," "My Nightgown and Slippers," and other
Humorous Works, Prose and Poetical, of GEORGE COLMAN.
With Life by G. B. BUCKSTONE, and Frontispiece by HOGARTH.

*" What antic have we here, in motley livery of red and yellow, with cap on
head, and dagger of lath in hand ? It is the king's jester, a professed droll,
strangely gifted in all grimace, who pulls faces, and sells grins by the yard.
For the impudent joke he has scarcely an equal."*—WESTMINSTER REVIEW.

Demy 8vo, cloth extra, with Coloured Illustrations and Maps, 21s.

Cope's History of the Rifle Brigade

(The Prince Consort's Own), formerly the 95th. By Sir WILLIAM
H. COPE, formerly Lieutenant Rifle Brigade.

Crown 8vo, cloth extra, gilt, with Portraits, 7s. 6d.

Creasy's Memoirs of Eminent Etonians ;

with Notices of the Early History of Eton College. By Sir
EDWARD CREASY, Author of "The Fifteen Decisive Battles of
the World." A New Edition, brought down to the Present
Time, with 13 Illustrations.

*" A new edition of ' Creasy's Etonians' will be welcome. The book was a
favourite a quarter of a century ago, and it has maintained its reputation. The
value of this new edition is enhanced by the fact that Sir Edward Creasy has
added to it several memoirs of Etonians who have died since the first edition
appeared. The work is eminently interesting."*—SCOTSMAN.

Crown 8vo, cloth gilt, two very thick Volumes, 7s. 6d. each.

Cruikshank's Comic Almanack.

Complete in Two SERIES: The FIRST from 1835 to 1843; the
SECOND from 1844 to 1853. A Gathering of the BEST HUMOUR
of THACKERAY, HOOD, MAYHEW, ALBERT SMITH, A'BECK-
ETT, ROBERT BROUGH, &c. With 2000 Woodcuts and Steel
Engravings by CRUIKSHANK, HINE, LANDELLS, &c.

To be Completed in Twenty-four Parts, quarto, at Five Shillings each,
profusely illustrated by Coloured and Plain Plates and Wood
Engravings,

The Cyclopædia of Costume;

or, A Dictionary of Dress—Regal, Ecclesiastical, Civil and Mili-
tary—from the Earliest Period in England to the reign of George
the Third. Including Notices of Contemporaneous Fashions on
the Continent, and preceded by a General History of the Costumes
of the Principal Countries of Europe. By J. R. PLANCHÉ,
Somerset Herald.— A Prospectus will be sent upon application.
Part XV. just ready.

*" There is no subject connected with dress with which ' Somerset Herald' is
not as familiar as ordinary men are with the ordinary themes of everyday life.
The gathered knowledge of many years is placed before the world in this his
latest work, and, when finished, there will exist no work on the subject half so
valuable. The numerous illustrations are all effective—for their accuracy the
author is responsible ; they are well drawn and well engraved, and, while in-
dispensable to a proper comprehension of the text, are satisfactory as works of
art."*—ART JOURNAL.

*" One of the most perfect works ever published upon the subject. . . . Beauti-
fully printed and superbly illustrated."*—STANDARD

*** *Part XIV. contains the Completion of the DICTIONARY, which,
as Vol. I. of the Book, forms a Complete Work in itself. This volume
may now be had, handsomely bound in half red morocco, gilt top, price
£3 13s. 6d. Cases for binding the volume may also be had, price 5s. each.*

*The remaining Parts will be occupied by the GENERAL HISTORY
OF THE COSTUMES OF EUROPE, arranged Chronologically.*

Crown 8vo, cloth extra, gilt and emblazoned, with Illustrations,
coloured and plain, 7s. 6d.

Cussans' Handbook of Heraldry.

With Instructions for Tracing Pedigrees and Deciphering Ancient
MSS.; Rules for the Appointment of Liveries, Chapters on
Continental and American Heraldry, &c. &c. By JOHN E.
CUSSANS. Illustrated with 360 Plates and Woodcuts.

Parts I. to X. now ready, 21*s.* each.

Cussans' History of Hertfordshire.

A County History, got up in a very superior manner, and ranging with the finest works of its class. By JOHN E. CUSSANS. Illustrated with full-page Plates on Copper and Stone, and a profusion of small Woodcuts.

" Mr. Cussans has, from sources not accessible to Clutterbuck, made most valuable additions to the manorial history of the county, from the earliest period downwards, cleared up many doubtful points, and given original details concerning various subjects untouched or imperfectly treated by that writer. The same may be said as to the lists of incumbents and the monumental inscriptions. Clutterbuck's errors and omissions have been carefully corrected and supplied, and the occurrences of the last fifty years added, so that we have these important features of the work complete: Particular attention has also been paid to the heraldry of the county. . . . The pedigrees seem to have been constructed with great care, and are a valuable addition to the genealogical history of the county. Mr. Cussans appears to have done his work conscientiously, and to have spared neither time, labour, nor expense to render his volumes worthy of ranking in the highest class of County Histories. The typography is entitled to unqualified praise, the paper, type, and illustrations being unexceptionable."— ACADEMY.

Demy 8vo, half-bound morocco, 21*s.*

Dibdin's Bibliomania ;

or, Book-Madness : A Bibliographical Romance. With numerous Illustrations. A New Edition, with a Supplement, including a Key to the Assumed Characters in the Drama.

*" I have not yet recovered from the delightful delirium into which your ' Bibliomania' has completely thrown me. Your book, to my taste, is one of the most extraordinary gratifications I have enjoyed for many years."—*ISAAC DISRAELI.

Two Vols., 8vo, cloth extra, 30*s.*

Dixon's White Conquest :

America in 1875. By W. HEPWORTH DIXON.

*" The best written, most instructive, and most entertaining book that Mr. Dixon has published since ' New America.' "—*ATHENÆUM.

SECOND EDITION, demy 8vo, cloth gilt, with Illustrations, 18*s.*

Dunraven's The Great Divide :

A Narrative of Travels in the Upper Yellowstone in the summer of 1874. By the EARL of DUNRAVEN. With Maps and numerous striking full-page Illustrations by VALENTINE W. BROMLEY.

*" There has not for a long time appeared a better book of travel than Lord Dunraven's ' The Great Divide.' . . . The book is full of clever observation, and both narrative and illustrations are thoroughly good."—*ATHENÆUM.

*" A jolly, rollicking narrative of adventure and sport, mixed up with a great deal of useful information concerning one of the most interesting regions in the American continent."—*NATURE.

Demy 8vo, cloth extra, with Illustrations, 24s.

Dodge's (Colonel) The Hunting Grounds

of the Great West: a Description of the Plains, Game, and Indians of the Great North American Desert. By RICHARD IRVING DODGE, Lieutenant-Colonel of the United States Army. With an Introduction by WILLIAM BLACKMORE; Map, and numerous Illustrations drawn by ERNEST GRISET.

Crown 8vo, cloth boards, 6s. per Volume ; a few Large Paper copies (only 50 printed), at 12s. per Vol.

Early English Poets.

Edited, with Introductions and Annotations, by the Rev. A. B. GROSART.

"Mr. Grosart has spent the most laborious and the most enthusiastic care on the perfect restoration and preservation of the text; and it is very unlikely that any other edition of the poet can ever be called for. . . From Mr. Grosart we always expect and always receive the final results of most patient and competent scholarship."—EXAMINER.

1. *Fletcher's (Giles, B.D.) Complete Poems:* Christ's Victorie in Heaven, Christ's Victorie on Earth, Christ's Triumph over Death, and Minor Poems. With Memorial-Introduction and Notes.

2. *Davies' (Sir John) Complete Poetical Works,* including Psalms I. to L. in Verse, and other hitherto Unpublished MSS., for the first time Collected and Edited. With Memorial-Introduction and Notes. Two Vols.

3. *Herrick's (Robert) Hes-*perides, Noble Numbers, and *Complete Collected Poems.* With Memorial-Introduction and Notes, Steel Portrait, Index of First Lines, and Glossarial Index, &c. Three Vols.

4. *Sidney's (Sir Philip) Complete Poetical Works,* including all those in "Arcadia." With Memorial-Introduction, Essay on the Poetry of Sidney, and Notes. [*In the press.*

5. *Donne's (Dr. John) Complete Poetical Works,* including the Satires and various from MSS. With Memorial-Introduction and Notes. [*In the press.*

** Other volumes are in active preparation.

Crown 8vo, cloth extra, gilt, with Illustrations, 6s.

Emanuel On Diamonds and Precious

Stones: their History, Value, and Properties ; with Simple Tests for ascertaining their Reality. By HARRY EMANUEL, F.R.G.S. With numerous Illustrations, Tinted and Plain.

Crown 8vo, cloth extra, with Illustrations, 7s. 6d.

The Englishman's House:

A Practical Guide to all interested in Selecting or Building a House, with full Estimates of Cost, Quantities, &c. By C. J. RICHARDSON. Third Edition. With nearly 600 Illustrations.

Crown 8vo, cloth extra, with Illustrations, 6s.

Fairholt's Tobacco:

Its History and Associations; including an Account of the Plant and its Manufacture; with its Modes of Use in all Ages and Countries. By F. W. FAIRHOLT, F.S.A. A New Edition, with Coloured Frontispiece and upwards of 100 Illustrations by the Author.

"*A very pleasant and instructive history of tobacco and its associations, which we cordially recommend alike to the votaries and to the enemies of the much-maligned but certainly not neglected weed. . . Full of interest and information.*"—DAILY NEWS.

"*A more complete and dainty book on a subject which some still think unsavoury it would not be easy to call to mind.*"—GRAPHIC.

Crown 8vo, cloth extra, with Illustrations, 4s. 6d.

Faraday's Chemical History of a Candle.

Lectures delivered to a Juvenile Audience. A New Edition. Edited by W. CROOKES, F.C.S. With numerous Illustrations.

Crown 8vo, cloth extra, with Illustrations, 4s. 6d.

Faraday's Various Forces of Nature.

A New Edition. Edited by W. CROOKES, F.C.S. With numerous Illustrations.

Crown 8vo, cloth extra, with Illustrations, 7s. 6d.

Finger-Ring Love:

Historical, Legendary, and Anecdotal.—Earliest Notices; Superstitions; Ring Investiture, Secular and Ecclesiastical; Betrothal and Wedding Rings; Ring-tokens; Memorial and Mortuary Rings; Posy-Rings; Customs and Incidents in Connection with Rings; Remarkable Rings, &c. By WILLIAM JONES, F.S.A. With Hundreds of Illustrations of Curious Rings of all Ages and Countries.

"*The book is both amusing and instructive.*"—DAILY TELEGRAPH.

"*Enters fully into the whole subject, and gives an amount of information and general reading in reference thereto which is of very high interest. The book is not only a sort of history of finger-rings, but is a collection of anecdotes in connection with them. . . . The volume is admirably illustrated, and altogether affords an amount of amusement and information which is not otherwise easily accessible.*"—SCOTSMAN.

"*One of those gossiping books which are as full of amusement as of instruction.*"—ATHENÆUM.

Demy 8vo, cloth extra, gilt, with Illustrations, 9s.

Figuier's Primitive Man :

A Popular Manual of the prevailing Theories of the Descent of Man, as promulgated by DARWIN, LYELL, Sir JOHN LUBBOCK, HUXLEY, E. B. TYLOR, and other eminent Ethnologists. Translated from the last French edition, and revised by E. B. T. With 263 Illustrations.

"*An interesting and essentially popular résumé of all that has been written on the subject. M. Figuier has collected together the evidences which modern researches have accumulated, and has done this with a considerable amount of care.*"—ATHENÆUM.

Demy 8vo, cloth extra, with Illustrations, 18s.

Gay's From Pall Mall to the Punjaub ;

or, With the Prince in India. By J. DREW GAY. With fine full-page Illustrations.

"*A lasting memorial of an interesting journey.*"—DAILY TELEGRAPH.

"*Written in a lively and unpretentious style, and sparkling here and there with genuine humour, the work is a decidedly attractive one.*"—LEEDS MERCURY.

"*A very readable and enjoyable narrative of a journey whose importance and interest are already part of history.*"—HOME NEWS.

Demy 8vo, cloth extra, gilt, with Illustrations, 18s.

Gell and Gandy's Pompeiana :

or, The Topography, Edifices, and Ornaments of Pompeii. With upwards of 100 Line Engravings by GOODALL, COOKE, HEATH, PYE, &c.

THE RUSKIN GRIMM.—Square crown 8vo, cloth extra, 6s. 6d.; gilt edges, 7s. 6d.

German Popular Stories.

Collected by the Brothers GRIMM, and Translated by EDGAR TAYLOR. Edited, with an Introduction, by JOHN RUSKIN. With 22 Illustrations after the inimitable designs of GEORGE CRUIKSHANK. Both Series Complete.

"*The illustrations of this volume . . . . are of quite sterling and admirable art, of a class precisely parallel in elevation to the character of the tales which they illustrate; and the original etchings, as I have before said in the Appendix to my 'Elements of Drawing,' were unrivalled in masterfulness of touch since Rembrandt (in some qualities of delineation, unrivalled even by him). . . . To make somewhat enlarged copies of them, looking at them through a magnifying glass, and never putting two lines where Cruikshank has put only one, would be an exercise in decision and severe drawing which would leave afterwards little to be learnt in schools.*"—Extract from Introduction by JOHN RUSKIN.

One Vol. crown 8vo, cloth extra, 9s.

Gilbert's (W. S.) Original Plays:

"A Wicked World," "Charity," "The Palace of Truth,"
"Pygmalion," "Trial by Jury," &c.

*" His workmanship is in its way perfect; it is very sound, very even, very
well sustained, and excellently balanced throughout."*—OBSERVER.

Demy 4to, cloth extra, with Illustrations, 31s. 6d.

Gillray the Caricaturist:

The Story of his Life and Times, with Anecdotal Descriptions of
his Engravings. Edited by THOMAS WRIGHT, Esq., M.A.,
F.S.A. With 83 full-page Plates, and numerous Wood
Engravings.

*" High as the expectations excited by this description [in the Introduction]
may be, they will not be disappointed. The most inquisitive or exacting reader
will find ready gathered to his hand, without the trouble of reference, almost every
scrap of narrative, anecdote, gossip, scandal, or epigram, that he can possibly
require for the elucidation of the caricatures."*—QUARTERLY REVIEW.

Crown 8vo, cloth extra, with a Map, 3s. 6d.

Gold;

Or, Legal Regulations for the Standard of Gold and Silver
Ware in the different Countries of the World. Translated from
the German of STÜDNITZ by Mrs. BREWER, and Edited, with
additions, by EDWIN W. STREETER.

Crown 8vo, cloth gilt and gilt edges, 7s. 6d.

The Golden Treasury of Thought:

AN ENCYCLOPÆDIA OF QUOTATIONS from Writers of all Times
and Countries. Selected and Edited by THEODORE TAYLOR.

Small 8vo, cloth gilt, 6s.

Gosse's King Erik:

A Tragedy. By EDMUND W. GOSSE. With a Vignette by W. B.
SCOTT.

*" The author's book, ' On Viol and Flute,' displayed such a remarkable ear for
music, such a singular poetic interpretation of flowers and trees, and such-like
children of Flora, and, above all, such a distinct and individual poetic savour,
that it would have been a pity indeed had these good gifts been wasted in any
wrong direction. In this case there is happily no cause for such pity. We have
seldom seen so marked an advance in a second book beyond a first. . . . The
faults of 'King Erik' are but slight matters; its merits are solid, and of a very
high order."*—ACADEMY.

Small 8vo, cloth gilt, 5s.

Gosse's On Viol and Flute.

Second Edition. With a Vignette by W. B. SCOTT.

Square 16mo, (Tauchnitz size), cloth extra,, 2s. per volume.

The Golden Library :

Bayard Taylor's Diver-
sions of the Echo Club.

The Book of Clerical Anec-
dotes.

Byron's Don Juan.

Carlyle (Thomas) on the
Choice of Books. With a Memoir. 1s. 6d.

Emerson's Letters and
Social Aims.

Godwin's (William) Lives
of the Necromancers.

Holmes's Autocrat of the
Breakfast Table. With an Introduction by G. A. SALA.

Holmes's Professor at the
Breakfast Table.

Hood's Whims and Oddi-
ties. Complete. With all the
original Illustrations.

Irving's   (Washington)
Tales of a Traveller.

Irving's   (Washington)
Tales of the Alhambra.

Jesse's (Edward) Scenes
and Occupations of Country Life.

Lamb's Essays of Elia.
Both Series Complete in One
Volume.

Leigh Hunt's Essays : A
Tale for a Chimney Corner, and
other Pieces. With Portrait,
and Introduction by EDMUND
OLLIER.

Mallory's (Sir Thomas)
Mort d'Arthur : The Stories of
King Arthur and of the Knights
of the Round Table. Edited by
B. MONTGOMERIE RANKING.

Pascal's Provincial Let-
ters. A New Translation, with
Historical Introduction and
Notes, by T. M'CRIE, D.D.,
LL.D.

Pope's Complete Poetical
Works.

Rochefoucauld's Maxims
and Moral Reflections. With
Notes, and an Introductory
Essay by SAINTE-BEUVE.

St. Pierre's Paul and
Virginia, and the Indian Cot-
tage. Edited, with Life, by the
Rev. E. CLARKE.

Shelley's   Early   Poems
and Queen Mab, with Essay by
LEIGH HUNT.

Shelley's Later Poems :
Laon and Cythna, &c.

Shelley's Posthumous
Poems, the Shelley Papers, &c.

Shelley's Prose Works,
including A Refutation of Deism,
Zastrozzi, St. Irvyne, &c.

White's Natural History
of Selborne. Edited, with additions, by THOMAS BROWN,
F.L.S.

' *A series of excellently printed and carefully annotated volumes, handy in size,*
nd altogether attractive.'—BOOKSELLER.

Crown 8vo, cloth extra, gilt, with Illustrations, 7s. 6d.

Greenwood's Low-Life Deeps.

An Account of the Strange Fish to be found there ; including "The Man and Dog Fight," with much additional and confirmatory evidence ; "With a Tally-Man," "A Fallen Star," "The Betting Barber," "A Coal Marriage," &c. By JAMES GREENWOOD. With Illustrations in tint by ALFRED CONCANEN.

"The book is interesting reading. It shows that there are many things in London life not dreamt of by most people. It is well got up, and contains a number of striking illustrations."—SCOTSMAN.

Crown 8vo, cloth extra, gilt, with Illustrations, 7s. 6d.

Greenwood's Wilds of London :

Descriptive Sketches, from Personal Observations and Experience, of Remarkable Scenes, People, and Places in London. By JAMES GREENWOOD. With 12 Tinted Illustrations by ALFRED CONCANEN.

"Mr. James Greenwood presents himself once more in the character of ' one whose delight it is to do his humble endeavour towards exposing and extirpating social abuses and those hole-and-corner evils which afflict society.' "—SATURDAY REVIEW.

Crown 8vo, cloth extra, gilt, with Illustrations, 4s. 6d.

Guyot's Earth and Man ;

Or, Physical Geography in its Relation to the History of Mankind. With Additions by Professors AGASSIZ, PIERCE, and GRAY. 12 Maps and Engravings on Steel, some Coloured, and a copious Index.

Crown 8vo, cloth extra, 6s.

Hake's New Symbols :

Poems. By THOMAS GORDON HAKE.

"The entire book breathes a pure and ennobling influence, shows welcome originality of idea and illustration, and yields the highest proof of imaginative faculty and mature power of expression."—ATHENÆUM.

Medium 8vo, cloth extra, gilt, with Illustrations, 7s. 6d.

Hall's (Mrs. S. C.) Sketches of Irish

Character. With numerous Illustrations on Steel and Wood by DANIEL MACLISE, Sir JOHN GILBERT, W. HARVEY, and G. CRUIKSHANK.

"The Irish sketches of this lady resemble Miss Mitford's beautiful English Sketches in ' Our Village,' but they are far more vigorous and picturesque and bright."—BLACKWOOD'S MAGAZINE.

Demy 8vo, cloth extra, with Portrait and Illustrations, 12s.

Hawker's Memorials :

Memorials of the late Rev. ROBERT STEPHEN HAWKER, some-time Vicar of Morwenstow, in the Diocese of Exeter. Collected, arranged, and edited by the Rev. FREDERICK GEORGE LEE, D.C.L., Vicar of All Saints', Lambeth. With Photographic Portrait, Pedigree, and Illustrations.

"*Dr. Lee's 'Memorials' is a far better record of Mr. Hawker, and gives a more reverent and more true idea of the man. . . . Dr. Lee rightly confines himself to his proper subject.*"—ATHENÆUM.

Two Vols. 8vo, cloth extra, with Illustrations, 36s.

Haydon's Correspondence & Table-Talk.

With a Memoir by his Son, FREDERIC WORDSWORTH HAYDON. Comprising a large number of hitherto Unpublished Letters from KEATS, WILKIE, SOUTHEY, WORDSWORTH, KIRKUP, LEIGH HUNT, LANDSEER, HORACE SMITH, Sir G. BEAUMONT, GOETHE, Mrs. SIDDONS, Sir WALTER SCOTT, TALFOURD, JEFFREY, Miss MITFORD, MACREADY, Mrs. BROWNING, LOCKHART, HALLAM, and others. With 23 Illustrations, including Facsimiles of many interesting Sketches, Portraits of HAYDON by KEATS and WILKIE, and HAYDON's Portraits of WILKIE, KEATS, and MARIA FOOTE.

"*There can, we think, be no question of its interest in a purely biographical sense, or of its literary merit. The letters and table-talk form a most valuable cont. ibution to the social and artistic history of the time.*"—PALL MALL GAZETTE.

"*The volumes are among the most interesting produced or likely to be produced in the present season.*"—EXAMINER.

"*Here we have a full-length portrait of a most remarkable man. . . . His son has done the work well—is clear and discriminating on the whole, and writes with ease and vigour. Over and above the interest that must be felt in Haydon himself, the letters afford us the opportunity of studying closely many of the greatest men and women of the time. . . . We do not hesitate to say that these letters and table-talk form a most valuable contribution to the history of art and literature in the past generation. The editor has selected and arranged them with uncommon judgment, adding many notes that contain ana and anecdotes. Every page has thus its point of interest. The book will no doubt have a wide audience, as it well deserves.*"—NONCONFORMIST.

Three Vols. royal 4to, cloth boards, £6 6s.; half-morocco, full gilt back and edges, £7 7s.

Historical Portraits ;

Upwards of 430 Engravings of Rare Prints. Comprising the Collections of RODD, RICHARDSON, CAULFIELD, &c. With Descriptive Text to every Plate, giving a brief outline of the most important Historical and Biographical Facts and Dates connected with each Portrait, and references to original Authorities.

Crown 8vo, cloth extra, gilt, 7s. 6d.

Hood's (Thomas) Choice Works,

In Prose and Verse. Including the CREAM OF THE COMIC ANNUALS. With Life of the Author, Portrait, and over Two Hundred original Illustrations.

"*Not only does the volume include the better-known poems by the author, but also what is happily described as 'the Cream of the Comic Annuals.' Such delicious things as 'Don't you smell Fire!' 'The Parish Revolution,' and 'Huggins and Duggins,' will never want readers.*"—GRAPHIC.

"*A fair representative selection of Hood's works, many of which have been hitherto inaccessible except at high prices. Most of the best known of his comic effusions—those punning ballads in which he has never been approached—are to be found in the liberal collection Messrs. Chatto & Windus have given to the public.*"—BIRMINGHAM DAILY MAIL.

Square crown 8vo, in a handsome and specially-designed binding, gilt edges, 6s.

Hood's (Tom) From Nowhere to the

North Pole: A Noah's Arkæological Narrative. With 25 Illustrations by W. BRUNTON and E. C. BARNES.

"*Poor Tom Hood! It is very sad to turn over the droll pages of 'From Nowhere to the North Pole,' and to think that he will never make the young people, for whom, like his famous father, he ever had such a kind, sympathetic heart, laugh or cry any more. This is a birthday story, and no part of it is better than the first chapter, concerning birthdays in general, and Frank's birthday in particular. The amusing letterpress is profusely interspersed with the jingling rhymes which children love and learn so easily. Messrs. Brunton and Barnes do full justice to the writer's meaning, and a pleasanter result of the harmonious co-operation of author and artist could not be desired.*"—TIMES.

Crown 8vo, cloth extra, gilt, 7s. 6d.

Hook's (Theodore) Choice Humorous

Works, including his Ludicrous Adventures, Bons-mots, Puns, and Hoaxes. With a new Life of the Author, Portraits, Facsimiles, and Illustrations.

"*His name will be preserved. His political songs and jeux d'esprit, when the hour comes for collecting them, will form a volume of sterling and lasting attraction; and after many clever romances of this age shall have sufficiently occupied public attention, and sunk, like hundreds of former generations, into utter oblivion, there are tales in his collection which will be read with even a greater interest than they commanded in their novelty.*"—J. G. LOCKHART.

Two Vols. royal 8vo, with Coloured Frontispieces, cloth extra, £2 5s.

Hope's Costume of the Ancients.

Illustrated in upwards of 320 Outline Engravings, containing Representations of Egyptian, Greek, and Roman Habits and Dresses.

"*The substance of many expensive works, containing all that may be necessary to give to artists, and even to dramatic performers and to others engaged in classical representations, an idea of ancient costumes sufficiently ample to prevent their offending in their performances by gross and obvious blunders.*"

Crown 8vo, cloth extra, 7s.

Horne's Orion:

An Epic Poem, in Three Books. By RICHARD HENGIST HORNE.
With Photographic Portrait. Tenth Edition.

"Orion will be admitted, by every man of genius, to be one of the noblest, if not the very noblest poetical work of the age. Its defects are trivial and conventional, its beauties intrinsic and supreme."—EDGAR ALLAN POE.

Atlas folio, half morocco gilt, £5 5s.

The Italian Masters:

Autotype Facsimiles of Original Drawings in the British Museum.
With Critical and Descriptive Notes, Biographical and Artistic,
by J. COMYNS CARR.

Crown 8vo, cloth extra, with Illustrations, 10s. 6d.

Jennings' The Rosicrucians:

Their Rites and Mysteries. With Chapters on the Ancient Fire
and Serpent Worshippers, and Explanations of Mystic Symbols
in Monuments and Talismans of Primæval Philosophers. By
HARGRAVE JENNINGS. With upwards of 300 Illustrations.

Small 8vo, cloth extra, 6s.

Jeux d'Esprit,

Written and Spoken, of the Later Wits and Humourists. Collected
and Edited by HENRY S. LEIGH.

Two Vols. 8vo, with 52 Illustrations and Maps, cloth extra, gilt, 14s.

Josephus's Complete Works.

Translated by WHISTON. Containing both "The Antiquities of
the Jews" and "The Wars of the Jews."

"This admirable translation far exceeds all preceding ones, and has never been equalled by any subsequent attempt of the kind."—LOWNDES.

Small 8vo, cloth, full gilt, gilt edges, with Illustrations, 6s.

Kavanaghs' Pearl Fountain,

And other Fairy Stories. By BRIDGET and JULIA KAVANAGH.
With Thirty Illustrations by J. MOYR SMITH.

Two Vols. crown 8vo, cloth extra, 21s.

Kingsley's Fireside Studies:

Essays. By HENRY KINGSLEY.

"These 'Fireside Studies' show Mr. Kingsley at his very best. Their pervading charms are their freshness and liveliness. The volumes are delightful."—TIMES.

Crown 8vo, cloth extra, gilt, with Portraits, 7s. 6d.

Lamb's Complete Works,

In Prose and Verse, reprinted from the Original Editions, with many Pieces hitherto unpublished. Edited, with Notes and Introduction, by R. H. SHEPHERD. With Two Portraits and Facsimile of a page of the "Essay on Roast Pig."

"*The genius of Mr. Lamb, as developed in his various writings, takes rank with the most original of the age. As a critic he stands facile princeps in the subjects he handled. Search English literature through, from its first beginnings until now, and you will find none like him. There is not a criticism he ever wrote that does not directly tell you a number of things you had no previous notion of. In criticism he was, indeed, in all senses of the word, a discoverer—like Vasco, Nunes, or Magellan. In that very domain of literature with which you fancied yourself most variously and closely acquainted, he would show you 'fresh fields and pastures new,' and these the most fruitful and delightful. For the riches he discovered were richer that they had lain so deep—the more valuable were they, when found, that they had eluded the search of ordinary men. As an essayist, Charles Lamb will be remembered in years to come with Rabelais and Montaigne, with Sir Thomas Browne, with Steele and with Addison. He unites many of the finest characteristics of these several writers. He has wisdom and wit of the highest order, exquisite humour, a genuine and cordial vein of pleasantry, and the most heart-touching pathos. In the largest acceptation of the word, he is a humanist.*"—JOHN FORSTER.

Crown 8vo, cloth extra, with numerous Illustrations, 10s. 6d.

Mary & Charles Lamb:

Their Poems, Letters and Remains. With Reminiscences and Notes by W. CAREW HAZLITT. With HANCOCK'S Portrait of the Essayist, Facsimiles of the Title-pages of the rare First Editions of Lamb's and Coleridge's Works, and numerous Illustrations.

"*Must be consulted by all future biographers of the Lambs.*"—DAILY NEWS.

"*Very many passages will delight those fond of literary trifles; hardly any portion will fail in interest for lovers of Charles Lamb and his sister.*"—STANDARD.

Post 8vo, cloth extra, with Portrait and Map, 9s.

Lee's (General) Life and Campaigns.

By his Nephew, EDWARD LEE CHILDE. With Steel-plate Portrait by JEENS, and a Map.

"*A valuable and well-written contribution to the history of the Civil War in the United States.*"—SATURDAY REVIEW.

"*As a clear and compendious survey of a life of the true heroic type, Mr. Childe's volume may well be commended to the English reader.*"—GRAPHIC.

Crown 8vo, cloth extra, with Illustrations, 7s. 6d.

Life in London;

Or, The History of Jerry Hawthorn and Corinthian Tom. With the whole of CRUIKSHANK's Illustrations, in Colours, after the Originals.

Demy 8vo, cloth extra, with Maps and Illustrations, 18s.

Lamont's Yachting in the Arctic Seas;

or, Notes of Five Voyages of Sport and Discovery in the Neighbourhood of Spitzbergen and Novaya Zemlya. By JAMES LAMONT, F.R.G.S. With numerous full-page Illustrations by Dr. LIVESAY.

"*After wading through numberless volumes of icy fiction, concocted narrative, and spurious biography of Arctic voyagers, it is pleasant to meet with a real and genuine volume. . . . He shows much tact in recounting his adventures, and they are so interspersed with anecdotes and information as to make them anything but wearisome. . . . The book, as a whole, is the most important addition made to our Arctic literature for a long time.*"—ATHENÆUM.

"*Full of entertainment and information.*"—NATURE.

Small crown 8vo, cloth extra, 4s. 6d.

Linton's Joshua Davidson,

Christian and Communist. By E. LYNN LINTON. Sixth Edition, with a New Preface.

"*In a short and vigorous preface, Mrs. Linton defends her notion of the logical outcome of Christianity as embodied in this attempt to conceive how Christ would have acted, with whom He would have fraternised, and who would have declined to receive Him, had He appeared in the present generation.*"—EXAMINER.

Crown 8vo, cloth extra, with Illustrations, 7s. 6d.

Longfellow's Complete Prose Works.

Including "Outre Mer," "Hyperion," "Kavanagh," "The Poets and Poetry of Europe," and "Driftwood." With Portrait and Illustrations by VALENTINE BROMLEY.

₊ This is by far the most complete edition ever issued in this country. "*Outre-Mer*" contains two additional chapters, restored from the first edition; while "*The Poets and Poetry of Europe*," and the little collection of Sketches entitled "*Driftwood*," are now first introduced to the English Public.

Crown 8vo, cloth extra, gilt, with Illustrations, 7s. 6d.

Longfellow's Poetical Works.

Carefully Reprinted from the Original Editions. With numerous fine Illustrations on Steel and Wood.

"*Mr. Longfellow has for many years been the best known and the most read of American poets; and his popularity is of the right kind, and rightly and fairly won. He has not stooped to catch attention by artifice, nor striven to force it by violence. His works have faced the test of parody and burlesque (which in these days is almost the common lot of writings of any mark), and have come off unharmed.*"—SATURDAY REVIEW.

Crown 8vo, cloth extra, 6s. 6d.

Lost Beauties of the English Language

An Appeal to Authors, Poets, Clergymen, and Public Speakers. By CHARLES MACKAY, LL.D.

THE FRASER PORTRAITS.—Demy 4to, cloth gilt and gilt edges, with 83 characteristic Portraits, 31s. 6d.

Maclise's Gallery of Illustrious Literary

Characters. With Notes by Dr. MAGINN. Edited, with copious Additional Notes, by WILLIAM BATES, B.A.

"*One of the most interesting volumes of this year's literature.*"—TIMES.
"*Deserves a place on every drawing-room table, and may not unfitly be removed from the drawing-room to the library.*"—SPECTATOR.

Crown 8vo, cloth extra, with Illustrations, 2s. 6d.

Madre Natura v. The Moloch of Fashion.

By LUKE LIMNER. With 32 Illustrations by the Author. FOURTH EDITION, revised and enlarged.

"*Agreeably written and amusingly illustrated. Common sense and erudition are brought to bear on the subjects discussed in it.*"—LANCET.

Handsomely printed in facsimile, price 5s.

Magna Charta.

An exact Facsimile of the Original Document in the British Museum, printed on fine plate paper, nearly 3 feet long by 2 feet wide, with the Arms and Seals of the Barons emblazoned in Gold and Colours.

*** A full Translation, with Notes, on a large sheet, 6d.

Small 8vo, cloth extra, 7s. 6d.

Mark Twain's Adventures of Tom Sawyer:

A Story.

"*The earlier part of the book is to our thinking the most amusing thing Mark Twain has written. The humour is not always uproarious, but it is always genuine, and sometimes almost pathetic.*"—ATHENÆUM.
"*A book to be read. There is a certain freshness and novelty about it, a practically romantic character, so to speak, which will make it very attractive.*"—SPECTATOR.
"*From a novel so replete with good things, and one so full of significance, as it brings before us what we can feel is the real spirit of home life in the Far West, there is no possibility of obtaining extracts which will convey to the reader any idea of the purport of the book. . . . The book will no doubt be a great favourite with boys, for whom it must in good part have been intended; but next to boys, we should say that it might be most prized by philosophers and poets.*"—EXAMINER.
"*Will delight all the lads who may get hold of it. We have made the experiment upon a youngster, and found that the reading of the book brought on constant peals of laughter.*"—SCOTSMAN.

Crown 8vo, cloth extra, with Illustrations, 7s. 6d.

Mark Twain's Choice Works.

Revised and Corrected throughout by the Author. With Life, Portrait, and numerous Illustrations.

Post 8vo, illustrated boards, 2s.

Mark Twain's Pleasure Trip on the

Continent of Europe. ("The Innocents Abroad," and "The New Pilgrim's Progress.")

Two Vols. crown 8vo, cloth extra, 18s.

Marston's (Dr. Westland) Dramatic
and Poetical Works. Collected Library Edition.

" The ' Patrician's Daughter' is an oasis in the desert of modern dramatic literature, a real emanation of mind. We do not recollect any modern work in which states of thought are so freely developed, except the ' Torquato Tasso' of Goethe. The play is a work of art in the same sense that a play of Sophocles is a work of art ; it is one simple idea in a state of gradual development . . . ' The Favourite of Fortune' is one of the most important additions to the stock of English prose comedy that has been made during the present century."—TIMES.

Crown 8vo, cloth extra, 8s.

Marston's (Philip B.) All in All:
Poems and Sonnets.

Crown 8vo, cloth extra, 8s.

Marston's (Philip B.) Song Tide,
And other Poems. Second Edition.

" This is a first work of extraordinary performance and of still more extraordinary promise. The youngest school of English poetry has received an important accession to its ranks in Philip Bourke Marston."—EXAMINER.

Crown 8vo, cloth extra, gilt, gilt edges, 7s. 6d.

Muses of Mayfair ;
Vers de Société of the Nineteenth Century. Including Selections from TENNYSON, BROWNING, SWINBURNE, ROSSETTI, JEAN INGELOW, LOCKER, INGOLDSBY, HOOD, LYTTON, C. S. C.; LANDOR, AUSTIN DOBSON, &c. Edited by H. C. PENNELL.

The National Gallery Illustrated.
Part I. THE BRITISH SCHOOL. With upwards of 100 Illustrations of the principal pictures at Trafalgar Square. Edited by HENRY BLACKBURN. Demy 8vo, uniform with "Academy Notes," 1s.   [Nearly Ready.

Crown 8vo, cloth extra, with Vignette Portraits, price 6s. per Vol.

The Old Dramatists :

Ben Jonson's Works.
With Notes, Critical and Explanatory, and a Biographical Memoir by WILLIAM GIFFORD. Edited by Col. CUNNINGHAM. Three Vols.

Chapman's Works.
Now First Collected. Complete in Three Vols. Vol. I. contains the Plays complete, including the doubtful ones ; Vol. II. the Poems and Minor Translations, with an Introductory Essay by

ALGERNON CHARLES SWINBURNE ; Vol. III. the Translations of the Iliad and Odyssey.

Marlowe's Works.
Including his Translations. Edited, with Notes and Introduction, by Col. CUNNINGHAM. One Vol.

Massinger's Plays.
From the Text of WILLIAM GIFFORD. With the addition of the Tragedy of "Believe as you List." Edited by Col. CUNNINGHAM. One Vol.

Fcap. 8vo, cloth extra, 6s.

O'Shaughnessy's (Arthur) An Epic of

Women, and other Poems. Second Edition.

Crown 8vo, cloth extra, 10s. 6d.

O'Shaughnessy's Lays of France.

(Founded on the "Lays of Marie.") Second Edition.

Fcap. 8vo, cloth extra, 7s. 6d.

O'Shaughnessy's Music and Moonlight :

Poems and Songs.

"It is difficult to say which is more exquisite, the technical perfection of structure and melody, or the delicate pathos of thought. Mr. O'Shaughnessy will enrich our literature with some of the very best songs written in our generation."—ACADEMY.

Crown 8vo, carefully printed on creamy paper, and tastefully bound in cloth for the Library, price 6s. each.

The Piccadilly Novels :

POPULAR STORIES BY THE BEST AUTHORS.

Antonina. By WILKIE COLLINS.
Illustrated by Sir J. GILBERT and ALFRED CONCANEN.

Basil. By WILKIE COLLINS.
Illustrated by Sir JOHN GILBERT and J. MAHONEY.

Hide and Seek. By WILKIE COLLINS.
Illustrated by Sir JOHN GILBERT and J. MAHONEY.

The Dead Secret. By WILKIE COLLINS.
Illustrated by Sir JOHN GILBERT and H. FURNISS.

Queen of Hearts. By WILKIE COLLINS.
Illustrated by Sir J. GILBERT and A. CONCANEN.

My Miscellanies. By WILKIE COLLINS.
With Steel Portrait, and Illustrations by A. CONCANEN.

The Woman in White. By WILKIE COLLINS.
Illustrated by Sir J. GILBERT and F. A. FRASER.

The Moonstone. By WILKIE COLLINS.
Illustrated by G. DU MAURIER and F. A. FRASER.

Man and Wife. By WILKIE COLLINS.
Illustrated by WILLIAM SMALL.

THE PICCADILLY NOVELS—*continued.*

Poor Miss Finch.
By WILKIE COLLINS.
Illustrated by G. Du MAURIER and EDWARD HUGHES.

Miss or Mrs.?
By WILKIE COLLINS.
Illustrated by S. L. FILDES and HENRY WOODS.

The New Magdalen.
By WILKIE COLLINS.
Illustrated by G. Du MAURIER and C. S. RANDS.

The Frozen Deep.
By WILKIE COLLINS.
Illustrated by G. Du MAURIER and J. MAHONEY.

The Law and the Lady.
By WILKIE COLLINS.
Illustrated by S. L. FILDES and S. HALL.

"*Like all the author's works, full of a certain power and ingenuity. . . . It is upon such suggestions of crime that the fascination of the story depends. . . . The reader feels it his duty to serve to the end upon the inquest on which he has been called by the author.*"—TIMES.

Felicia.
By M. BETHAM EDWARDS.
With a Frontispiece by W. BOWLES.

"*A noble novel. Its teaching is elevated, its story is sympathetic, and the kind of feeling its perusal leaves behind is that more ordinarily derived from music or poetry than from prose fiction. Few works in modern fiction stand as high in our estimation as this.*"—SUNDAY TIMES.

Patricia Kemball.
By E. LYNN LINTON.
With Frontispiece by G. Du MAURIER.

"*A very clever and well-constructed story, original and striking, interesting all through. A novel abounding in thought and power and interest.*"—TIMES.
"*Displays genuine humour, as well as keen social observation. Enough graphic portraiture and witty observation to furnish materials for half-a-dozen novels of the ordinary kind.*"—SATURDAY REVIEW.

The Atonement of Leam Dundas.
By E. LYNN LINTON.
With a Frontispiece by HENRY WOOD.

"*In her narrowness and her depth, in her boundless loyalty, her self-forgetting passion, that exclusiveness of love which is akin to cruelty, and the fierce humility which is vicarious pride, Leam Dundas is a striking figure. In one quality the authoress has in some measure surpassed herself.*"—PALL MALL GAZETTE.

The Evil Eye, and other Stories.
By KATHARINE S. MACQUOID.
Illustrated by THOMAS R. MACQUOID and PERCY MACQUOID.

"*For Norman country life what the 'Johnny Ludlow' stories are for English rural delineation, that is, cameos delicately, if not very minutely or vividly wrought, and quite finished enough to give a pleasurable sense of artistic ease and faculty. A word of commendation is merited by the illustrations.*"—ACADEMY.

Number Seventeen.
By HENRY KINGSLEY.

Oakshott Castle.
By HENRY KINGSLEY.
With a Frontispiece by SHIRLEY HODSON.

"*A brisk and clear north wind of sentiment—sentiment that braces instead of enervating—blows through all his works, and makes all their readers at once healthier and more glad.*"—SPECTATOR.

THE PICCADILLY NOVELS—*continued.*

Open! Sesame!
By FLORENCE MARRYAT.
Illustrated by F. A. FRASER.

" *A story which arouses and sustains the reader's interest to a higher degree than, perhaps, any of its author's former works. . . . A very excellent story.*"—GRAPHIC.

Whiteladies.
By Mrs. OLIPHANT.
With Illustrations by A. HOPKINS and H. WOODS.

" *Is really a pleasant and readable book, written with practical ease and grace.*"—TIMES.

The Best of Husbands.
By JAMES PAYN.
Illustrated by J. MOYR SMITH.

Walter's Word.
By JAMES PAYN.
Illustrated by J. MOYR SMITH.

Halves.
By JAMES PAYN.
With a Frontispiece by J. MAHONEY.

" *His novels are always commendable in the sense of art. They also possess another distinct claim to our liking : the girls in them are remarkably charming and true to nature, as most people, we believe, have the good fortune to observe nature represented by girls.*"—SPECTATOR.

The Way we Live Now.
By ANTHONY TROLLOPE.
With Illustrations.

" *Mr. Trollope has a true artist's idea of tone, of colour, of harmony : his pictures are one, and seldom out of drawing ; he never strains after effect, is fidelity itself in expressing English life, is never guilty of caricature.*"—FORTNIGHTLY REVIEW.

Diamond Cut Diamond.
By T. A. TROLLOPE.

" *The indefinable charm of Tuscan and Venetian life breathes in his pages.*" —TIMES.

" *Full of life, of interest, of close observation, and sympathy. . . . When Mr. Trollope paints a scene it is sure to be a scene worth painting.*"—SATURDAY REVIEW.

Bound to the Wheel.
By JOHN SAUNDERS.

Guy Waterman.
By JOHN SAUNDERS.

One Against the World.
By JOHN SAUNDERS.

The Lion in the Path.
By JOHN SAUNDERS.

" *A carefully written and beautiful story—a story of goodness and truth, which is yet as interesting as though it dealt with the opposite qualities. . . . The author of this really clever story has been at great pains to work out all its details with elaborate conscientiousness, and the result is a very vivid picture of the ways of life and habits of thought of a hundred and fifty years ago. . . . Certainly a very interesting book.*"—TIMES.

Crown 8vo, red cloth, extra, 5s. each.

Ouida's Novels.—Uniform Edition.

Folle Farine.	By OUIDA.	Pascarel.	By OUIDA.
Idalia.	By OUIDA.	Puck.	By OUIDA.
Chandos.	By OUIDA.	Dog of Flanders.	By OUIDA.
Under Two Flags.	By OUIDA.	Strathmore.	By OUIDA.
Tricotrin.	By OUIDA.	Two Little Wooden Shoes.	By OUIDA.
Cecil Castlemaine's Gage.	By OUIDA.	Signa.	By OUIDA.
Held in Bondage.	By OUIDA.	In a Winter City.	By OUIDA.

"*Keen poetic insight, an intense love of nature, a deep admiration of the beautiful in form and colour, are the gifts of Ouida.*"—MORNING POST.

Mr. WILKIE COLLINS'S NEW NOVEL.—Two Vols. crown 8vo, 21s.

The Two Destinies:

A Romance. By WILKIE COLLINS, Author of "The Woman in White."

"*His ability as a story-teller is shown in the skill with which he holds the reader's attention through a long series of nonsense history. The book is sure to be popular, and deserves to be so for its literary merits.*"—TIMES.

"*Curious, clever, here and there of absorbing interest.*"—NONCONFORMIST.

"*As full of absorbing interest as 'The Woman in White.' With practised art and all his old lucidity of style, Mr. Collins excites the reader's interest in the very first chapter. A strong vein of the supernatural runs through 'The Two Destinies,' which cannot fail to be read with intense interest.*"—ILLUSTRATED NEWS.

NEW NOVEL BY Dr. SANDWITH.—Three Vols. cr. 8vo, 31s. 6d.

Minsterborough:

A Tale of English Life. By HUMPHRY SANDWITH, C.B., D.C.L.

"*It is a long time since we have read anything so refreshing as the novel to the composition of which Mr. Sandwith has been devoting such time and labour as could be spared from the more serious duties of an apostle of Democracy and clean water. Everything in the book is so delightfully straightforward. We are never bothered with subtle analysis of character, or with dark suggestions that things are other than they seem. . . . The story is not at all badly told.*"—ATHENÆUM.

JEAN MIDDLEMASS'S NEW NOVEL.—Three Vols. crown 8vo, 31s. 6d.

Mr. Dorillion:

A Novel. By JEAN MIDDLEMASS, Author of "Wild Georgie."

"*This is quite the best novel which Miss Middlemass has written. The story is well conceived, well told, full of strong situations, and rich in surprises; the characters speak, act, and think like human beings, and the style is uniformly lively and well sustained.*"—WORLD.

A New Writer.—Three Vols. crown 8vo, 31s. 6d.

The Democracy:

A Novel. By WHYTE THORNE.

"*A very careful, and in many respects very praiseworthy story.*"—SATURDAY REVIEW.

"*It is always difficult for anyone not personally concerned in English politics to write about them without making serious blunders; but the author of the novel before us keeps clear of error, and writes pleasantly enough.*"—ATHENÆUM.

MRS. MACQUOID'S NEW NOVEL.—Three Vols. crown 8vo, 31s. 6d.

Lost Rose;

and other Stories. By KATHARINE S. MACQUOID.

T. A. TROLLOPE'S NEW NOVEL.—Three Vols. crown 8vo, 31s. 6d.

A Family Party in the Piazza of

St. Peter's. By T. ADOLPHUS TROLLOPE. [*In the press.*

NEW NOVEL BY JAMES GREENWOOD.—3 vols. crown 8vo, 31s. 6d.

Dick Temple.

By JAMES GREENWOOD. [*In the press.*

Two Vols. 8vo, cloth extra, with Illustrations, 10s. 6d.

Plutarch's Lives of Illustrious Men.

Translated from the Greek, with Notes Critical and Historical, and a Life of Plutarch, by JOHN and WILLIAM LANGHORNE. New Edition, with Medallion Portraits.

"*When I write, I care not to have books about me; but I can hardly be without a 'Plutarch.'*"—MONTAIGNE.

Crown 8vo, cloth extra, with Portrait and Illustrations, 7s. 6d.

Poe's Choice Prose and Poetical Works.

With BAUDELAIRE'S "Essay."

"*Poe's great power lay in writing tales, which rank in a class by themselves, and have their characteristics strongly defined.*"—FRASER'S MAGAZINE.

"*Poe stands as much alone among verse-writers as Salvator Rosa among painters.*"—SPECTATOR.

Small 8vo, cloth extra, with Illustrations, 3s. 6d.

The Prince of Argolis:

A Story of the Old Greek Fairy Time. By J. MOYR SMITH. With 130 Illustrations by the Author.

Crown 8vo, cloth extra, with Portrait and Facsimile, 12s. 6d.

The Final Reliques of Father Prout.

Collected and Edited, from MSS. supplied by the family of the Rev. FRANCIS MAHONY, by BLANCHARD JERROLD.

" We heartily commend this handsome volume to all lovers of sound wit, genuine humour, and manly sense."—SPECTATOR.

" Sparkles all over, and is full of interest. Mahony, like Sydney Smith, could write on no subject without being brilliant and witty."—BRITISH QUARTERLY REVIEW.

" It is well that the present long-delayed volume should remind a younger generation of his fame. . . . The charming letters from Paris, Florence, and Rome . . . are the most perfect specimens of what a foreign correspondence ought to be."—ACADEMY.

In Two Series, small 4to, blue and gold, gilt edges, 6s. each.

Puniana ;

or, Thoughts Wise and Other-Why's. A New Collection of Riddles, Conundrums, Jokes, Sells, &c. In Two Series, each containing 3000 of the best Riddles, 10,000 most outrageous Puns, and upwards of Fifty beautifully executed Drawings by the Editor, the Hon. HUGH ROWLEY. Each Series is complete in itself.

" A witty, droll, and most amusing work, profusely and elegantly illustrated." —STANDARD.

Crown 8vo, cloth extra, gilt, 7s. 6d.

The Pursuivant of Arms ;

or, Heraldry founded upon Facts. A Popular Guide to the Science of Heraldry. By J. R. PLANCHÉ, Esq., Somerset Herald. To which are added, Essays on the BADGES OF THE HOUSES OF LANCASTER AND YORK. With Coloured Frontispiece, five full-page Plates, and about 200 Illustrations.

Crown 8vo, cloth extra, 7s. 6d.

Rabelais' Works.

Faithfully Translated from the French, with variorum Notes, and numerous Characteristic Illustrations by GUSTAVE DORÉ.

Handsomely printed, price 5s.

The Roll of Battle Abbey ;

Or, a List of the Principal Warriors who came over from Normandy with William the Conqueror, and Settled in this Country, A.D. 1066-7. Printed on fine plate paper, nearly three feet by two, with the principal Arms emblazoned in Gold and Colours.

In 4to, very handsomely printed, extra gold cloth, 12s.

The Roll of Caerlaverock,

The Oldest Heraldic Roll ; including the Original Anglo-Norman Poem, and an English Translation of the MS. in the British Museum. By THOMAS WRIGHT, M.A. The Arms emblazoned in Gold and Colours.

NEW AND POPULAR EDITION OF "SANSON'S MEMOIRS."—One Vol. crown 8vo, cloth extra, 7s. 6d.

Memoirs of the Sanson Family :

Seven Generations of Executioners. By HENRI SANSON. Translated from the French, with an Introduction, by CAMILLE BARRÈRE.

"*A faithful translation of this curious work, which will certainly repay perusal —not on the ground of its being full of horrors, for the original author seems to be rather ashamed of the technical aspect of his profession, and is commendably reticent as to its details, but because it contains a lucid account of the most notable causes célèbres from the time of Louis XIV. to a period within the memory of persons still living. . . . Can scarcely fail to be extremely entertaining.*"— DAILY TELEGRAPH.

Crown 8vo, cloth extra, profusely Illustrated, 4s. 6d. each.

The "Secret Out" Series.

The Volumes are as follows :

The Art of Amusing :

A Collection of Graceful Arts, Games, Tricks, Puzzles, and Charades. By FRANK BELLEW. 300 Illustrations.

Hanky-Panky :

Very Easy Tricks, Very Difficult Tricks, White Magic, Sleight of Hand. Edited by W. H. CREMER. 200 Illustrations.

Magician's Own Book :

Performances with Cups and Balls, Eggs, Hats, Handkerchiefs, &c. All from Actual Experience. Edited by W. H. CREMER. 200 Illustrations.

Magic No Mystery.

Tricks with Cards, Dice, Balls, &c., with fully descriptive Directions ; the Art of Secret Writing ; the Training of Performing Animals, &c. With Coloured Frontispiece and many Illustrations.

The Merry Circle :

A Book of New Intellectual Games and Amusements. By CLARA BELLEW. Many Illustrations.

The Secret Out :

One Thousand Tricks with Cards, and other Recreations ; with Entertaining Experiments in Drawing-room or "White Magic." By W. H. CREMER. 300 Engravings.

Post 8vo, with Illustrations, cloth extra, gilt edges, 18s.

The Lansdowne Shakespeare.

Beautifully printed in red and black, in small but very clear type. With engraved facsimile of DROESHOUT'S Portrait, and 37 beautiful Steel Plates, after STOTHARD.

In reduced facsimile, small 8vo, half Roxburghe, 10s. 6d.

The First Folio Shakespeare.

Mr. WILLIAM SHAKESPEARE'S Comedies, Histories, and Tragedies. Published according to the true Originall Copies. London, Printed by ISAAC IAGGARD and ED. BLOUNT, 1623.—An exact Reproduction of the extremely rare original, in reduced facsimile by a photographic process—ensuring the strictest accuracy in every detail. *A full prospectus will be sent upon application.*

"*To Messrs. Chatto and Windus belongs the merit of having done more to facilitate the critical study of the text of our great dramatist than all the Shakespeare clubs and societies put together. A complete facsimile of the celebrated First Folio edition of 1623 for half-a-guinea is at once a miracle of cheapness and enterprise. Being in a reduced form, the type is necessarily rather diminutive, but it is as distinct as in a genuine copy of the original, and will be found to be as useful and far more handy to the student than the latter.*"—ATHENÆUM.

Two Vols. crown 8vo, cloth extra, 18s.

The School of Shakespeare.

Including "The Life and Death of Captain Thomas Stukeley," with a New Life of Stucley, from Unpublished Sources; "A Warning for Fair Women," with a Reprint of the Account of the Murder; "Nobody and Somebody;" "The Cobbler's Prophecy;" "Histriomastix;" "The Prodigal Son," &c. Edited, with Introductions and Notes, by RICHARD SIMPSON.

Crown 8vo, cloth extra, gilt, with 10 full-page Tinted Illustrations, 7s. 6d.

Sheridan's Complete Works,

with Life and Anecdotes. Including his Dramatic Writings, printed from the Original Editions, his Works in Prose and Poetry, Translations, Speeches, Jokes, Puns, &c.; with a Collection of Sheridaniana.

"*The editor has brought together within a manageable compass not only the seven plays by which Sheridan is best known, but a collection also of his poetical pieces which are less familiar to the public, sketches of unfinished dramas, selections from his reported witticisms, and extracts from his principal speeches. To these is prefixed a short but well-written memoir, giving the chief facts in Sheridan's literary and political career; so that, with this volume in his hand, the student may consider himself tolerably well furnished with all that is necessary for a general comprehension of the subject of it.*"—PALL MALL GAZETTE.

Crown 8vo, cloth extra, with Illustrations, 7s. 6d.

Signboards;

Their History. With Anecdotes of Famous Taverns and Remarkable Characters. By JACOB LARWOOD and JOHN CAMDEN HOTTEN. With nearly 100 Illustrations.

"*Even if we were ever so maliciously inclined, we could not pick out all Messrs. Larwood and Hotten's plums, because the good things are so numerous as to defy the most wholesale depredation.*"—TIMES.

Crown 8vo, cloth extra, gilt, 6*s.* 6*d.*

The Slang Dictionary;

Etymological, Historical, and Anecdotal. An ENTIRELY NEW EDITION, revised throughout, and considerably Enlarged.

" *We are glad to see the Slang Dictionary reprinted and enlarged. From a high scientific point of view this book is not to be despised. Of course it cannot fail to be amusing also. It contains the very vocabulary of unrestrained humour, and oddity, and grotesqueness. In a word, it provides valuable material both for the student of language and the student of human nature.*"—ACADEMY.

Exquisitely printed in miniature, cloth extra, gilt edges, 2*s.* 6*d.*

The Smoker's Text-Book.

By J. HAMER, F.R.S.L.

Crown 8vo, cloth extra, 9*s.*

Stedman's Victorian Poets:

Critical Essays. By EDMUND CLARENCE STEDMAN.

" *We ought to be thankful to those who do critical work with competent skill and understanding, with honesty of purpose, and with diligence and thoroughness of execution. And Mr. Stedman, having chosen to work in this line, deserves the thanks of English scholars by these qualities and by something more ; . . . he is faithful, studious, and discerning.*"—SATURDAY REVIEW.

Imperial 4to, containing 150 beautifully-finished full-page Engravings and Nine Vignettes, all tinted, and some illuminated in gold and colours, half-morocco, £9 9*s.*

Stothard's Monumental Effigies of Great

Britain. With Historical Description and Introduction, by JOHN KEMPE, F.S.A. A NEW EDITION, with a large body of Additional Notes by JOHN HEWITT.

" *A new edition of Stothard is quite an era in Archæology, and we welcome it the more because two of the most industrious members of the Archæological Institute have contributed greatly to its augmentation and improvement. The work has been reproduced by Messrs. Chatto & Windus, with many additional notes by Mr. Hewitt. In order to the production of these notes, Mr. Hewitt visited almost all the monuments drawn by Stothard, and the result of his examinations was a constant subject of discussion between himself and Mr. Albert Way, to which we owe the large amount of additamenta in the new edition now before us. To Stothard's work, more than to any other, may perhaps be attributed the great revival of taste and feeling for the monuments of our ancestors which the present generation has seen. The interest of the subject is of the most universal character, and this new edition of Stothard is sure to be very popular. It will be a great satisfaction to our readers to find that the result of recent Archæological Investigations upon such subjects have been carefully brought together in the work under consideration. Besides the exhaustive account of the effigies themselves, the work as it now stands includes a concise history of mediæval costume, of monumental architecture, sculpture, brass engraving, and the numerous topics arising from the review of a series of examples extending from the twelfth to the sixteeth century. Foreign as well as English monuments have been used to illustrate the numerous points discussed in the work.*"—ARCHÆOLOGICAL JOURNAL, June, 1876.

. A few Large Paper copies, royal folio, with the arms illuminated in gold and colours, and the plates very carefully finished in body-colours, heightened with gold in the very finest style, half-morocco, £15 15*s.*

Crown 8vo, cloth extra, gilt edges, with Illustrations, 7s. 6d.

Thomson's Seasons and Castle of In-

dolence. With a Biographical and Critical Introduction by ALLAN CUNNINGHAM, and over 50 fine Illustrations on Steel and Wood.

Crown 4to, cloth extra, gilt and gilt edges, with Illustrations, 21s.

Thornbury's Historical and Legendary

Ballads and Songs. Illustrated by J. WHISTLER, JOHN TEN-NIEL, A. F. SANDYS, W. SMALL, M. J. LAWLESS, J. D. WATSON, G. J. PINWELL, F. WALKER, and others.

"*Mr. Thornbury has perceived with laudable clearness that one great requisite of poetry is that it should amuse. He rivals Goethe in the variety and startling incidents of his ballad-romances; he is full of vivacity and spirit, and his least impassioned pieces ring with a good out-of-doors music of sword and shield. Some of his mediæval poems are particularly rich in colour and tone. The old Norse ballads, too, are worthy of great praise. Best of all, however, we like his Cavalier songs; there is nothing of the kind in English more spirited, masculine, and merry.*"—ACADEMY.

"*Will be welcomed by all true lovers of art. . . . We must be grateful that so many works of a school distinguished for its originality should be collected into a single volume.*"—SATURDAY REVIEW.

Crown 8vo, cloth extra, 10s. 6d.

Cyril Tourneur's Collected Works,

including a unique Poem, entitled "The Transformed Metamorphosis;" and "Laugh and Lie Down, or, the World's Folly." Now first Collected, and Edited, with Critical Preface, Introductions, and Notes, by J. CHURTON COLLINS. [*In the press.*

Crown 8vo, cloth extra, with Illustrations, 7s. 6d.

J. M. W. Turner's Life and Correspond-

ence. Founded upon Letters and Papers furnished by his Friends and fellow Academicians. By WALTER THORNBURY. A New Edition, entirely rewritten and considerably enlarged. With numerous Illustrations in colours, facsimiled from Turner's original Drawings.

Crown 8vo, cloth extra, with Illustrations, 7s. 6d.

Timbs' Clubs and Club Life in London.

With Anecdotes of its famous Coffee-houses, Hostelries, and Taverns. By JOHN TIMBS, F.S.A. With numerous Illustrations.

"*The book supplies a much-felt want. The club is the avenue to general society of the present day, and Mr. Timbs gives the entrée to the club. The scholar and antiquary will also find the work a repertory of information on many disputed points of literary interest, and especially respecting various well-known anecdotes, the value of which only increases with the lapse of time.*"—MORNING POST.

Crown 8vo, cloth extra, with Illustrations, 7s. 6d.

Timbs' English Eccentrics and Eccentricities :

Stories of Wealth and Fashion, Delusions, Impostures, and Fanatic Missions, Strange Sights and Sporting Scenes, Eccentric Artists, Theatrical Folks, Men of Letters, &c. By JOHN TIMBS, F.S.A. With nearly 50 Illustrations.

" The reader who would fain enjoy a harmless laugh in some very odd company might do much worse than take an occasional dip into ' English Eccentrics.' The illustrations are admirably suited to the letterpress."—GRAPHIC.

Crown 4to, half-Roxburghe, 12s. 6d.

Vagabondiana ;

or, Anecdotes of Mendicant Wanderers through the Streets of London ; with Portraits of the most Remarkable, drawn from the Life by JOHN THOMAS SMITH, late Keeper of the Prints in the British Museum. With Introduction by FRANCIS DOUCE, and Descriptive Text. With the Woodcuts and the 32 Plates, from the original Coppers.

Large crown 8vo, cloth antique, with Illustrations, 7s. 6d.

Walton and Cotton's Complete Angler ;

Or, The Contemplative Man's Recreation : being a Discourse of Rivers, Fish-ponds, Fish and Fishing, written by IZAAK WALTON ; and Instructions how to Angle for a Trout or Grayling in a clear Stream, by CHARLES COTTON. With Original Memoirs and Notes by Sir HARRIS NICOLAS, K.C.M.G. With the 61 Plate Illustrations, precisely as in Pickering's two-volume Edition.

" Among the reprints of the year, few will be more welcome than this edition of the 'Complete Angler,' with Sir Harris Nicolas's Memoirs, and Notes, and Stothards and Inskipp's illustrations."—SATURDAY REVIEW.

Crown 8vo, cloth extra, with Vignette Portrait, 9s.

Wells' Joseph and his Brethren :

A Dramatic Poem. By CHARLES WELLS. With an Introductory Essay by ALGERNON CHARLES SWINBURNE.

" The author of ' Joseph and his Brethren' will some day have to be acknowledged among the memorable men of the second great period in our poetry. . . There are lines even in the overture of his poem which might, it seems to me, more naturally be mistaken even by an expert in verse for the work of the young Shakspeare, than any to be gathered elsewhere in the fields of English poetry."—SWINBURNE.

" In its combination of strength and delicacy, in sweet liquid musical flow, in just cadence, and in dramatic incisiveness of utterance, the language throughout keeps closer to the level of the Elizabethan dramatists than that of any dramatist of subsequent times."—ATHENÆUM.

Carefully printed on paper to imitate the Original, 22 in. by 14 in., price 5s.

The Warrant to Execute Charles I.

An exact Facsimile of this important Document, with the Fifty-nine Signatures of the Regicides, and corresponding Seals.

Beautifully printed on paper to imitate the Original MS., price 2s.

Warrant to Execute Mary Q. of Scots.

An exact Facsimile, including the Signature of Queen Elizabeth, and a Facsimile of the Great Seal.

In portfolios, price £4 4s. each series.

Wild's Cathedrals.

Select Examples of the Ecclesiastical Architecture of the Middle Ages; arranged in Two Series (the First FOREIGN, the Second ENGLISH). Each Series containing Twelve fine Plates, mounted upon Cardboard, and carefully Coloured, after the Original Drawings, by CHARLES WILD.

Three Vols. 8vo, with 103 Plates, exhibiting nearly four hundred figures of Birds, accurately engraved and beautifully printed in Colours, cloth extra, gilt, £3 3s.

Wilson's American Ornithology;

or, Natural History of the Birds of the United States; with the Continuation by Prince CHARLES LUCIAN BONAPARTE. New and Enlarged Edition, completed by the insertion of above One Hundred Birds omitted in the Original Work, and Illustrated by valuable Notes, and a Life of the Author, by Sir WILLIAM JARDINE.

"*The History of American Birds, by Alexander Wilson, is equal in elegance to the most distinguished of our own splendid works on Ornithology.*"—CUVIER.

*** Also a few Large Paper copies, 4to, with the Plates all carefully Coloured by hand, at £6 6s.

Crown 8vo, cloth extra, with Illustrations, 7s. 6d.

Wright's Caricature History of the

Georges. (*The House of Hanover.*) With 400 Pictures, Caricatures, Squibs, Broadsides, Window Pictures, &c. By THOMAS WRIGHT, Esq., M.A., F.S.A.

"*Emphatically one of the liveliest of books, as also one of the most interesting. Has the twofold merit of being at once amusing and edifying.*"—MORNING POST.

Large post 8vo, cloth extra, gilt, with Illustrations, 7s. 6d.

Wright's History of Caricature and of

the Grotesque in Art, Literature, Sculpture, and Painting, from the Earliest Times to the Present Day. By THOMAS WRIGHT, M.A., F.S.A. Profusely illustrated by F. W. FAIRHOLT, F.S.A.

"*A very amusing and instructive volume.*"—SATURDAY REVIEW.

J. OGDEN AND CO., PRINTERS, 172, ST. JOHN STREET, E.C.

www.ingramcontent.com/pod-product-compliance
Lightning Source LLC
Chambersburg PA
CBHW020353030726
47496CB00007B/2126